# Blood, Secrets and Lies 2 The Grave

## Ingrid Crayton

# Table of Contents

Prologue. . . . . . . . . . . . . . . . . . . . . . . . . . . . . . iv

The Family. . . . . . . . . . . . . . . . . . . . . . . . . . . . 1

Who Did It?. . . . . . . . . . . . . . . . . . . . . . . . . . 17

Familiy Get Together . . . . . . . . . . . . . . . . . . . 43

Wasn't Me . . . . . . . . . . . . . . . . . . . . . . . . . . . 67

No Party For Me . . . . . . . . . . . . . . . . . . . . . . 85

Those Eyes . . . . . . . . . . . . . . . . . . . . . . . . . . 101

Flashback. . . . . . . . . . . . . . . . . . . . . . . . . . . 121

Fire. . . . . . . . . . . . . . . . . . . . . . . . . . . . . . . . 129

Acknowledgments . . . . . . . . . . . . . . . . . . . . 159

# Prologue

Being the owner of two salons is a lot of work, especially when you're trying to find the right employees. I had to clean the house which isn't always easy. I had one stylist tell me she didn't need anyone watchin' over her. I had to tell that young tramp, "There's the door." Of course, she wasn't expecting that. About a week later she calls beggin' me to come back. But I said, "No." I don't do drama, at least not at my place of business. It took a while but now I have a second salon that I can be proud of. But most importantly I'm proud of my family. We have more drama than most families but when the shit hits the fan, my family falls into formation like soldiers ready to fight. Let me introduce myself again, I'm Renee the oldest of three girls. I'm the protector of the family at least in my mind. Oh, excuse me the second oldest of four girls now. Who would've thought? I'll explain in a minute. The age of thirteen is a big deal to the women in our family. Our bloodline carries unique gifts passed down through our ancestors. We can control the wind, rain and fire. We can stop a human heart in an instant. Along with controlling nature, we have the power to cast spells or chants to help and heal or to ultimately kill. Are these gifts or a curse? But there are consequences to the use of our gifts. Can we do the worse to the worse and get away with it? The answer to most people would be yes but we're not most people. We still must be accountable for the gifts that were given to us by the Lord. But some may say these gifts are not of God. But that's not my battle. I know who I am. I still must stand before God on judgment day like everyone else. I pray my name is in the Book of the Lambs. But because of some of the crazy shit I did and my family, that remains to be seen. Notice how I say, "Gifts". Some may say our gifts are evil. Since the beginning of time, all the women in our family have been called witches, voodoo priests, devil worshipers and even sorcerers. We're just like everyone else. We were born in Georgia but raised with creole love in Louisiana where my parents and most of my family are from. People think they know us. But they really don't, until they cross us. This is our family story, once again.

# Chapter One

## The Family

So much has happened in the past couple of years. Where do I begin? On what was supposed to be my wedding day, turned out to be a day of uncertainty and a day that my faith was tested. I'm not talkin' about I got cold feet, or the caterers were a no-show. Shit, that's easy. Someone from my past decided to take matters into their own hands. It was my ex-boyfriend, Jonathan who didn't know how to move on. Jonathan thought no one deserved me but him. Jonathan stabbed Eric, my husband, the day of our wedding while he was getting dressed. I was devastated, scared, helpless and angry. Seeing Eric lying there in the hospital bed unresponsive made me question God. I asked, "How could God let something like this happen to Eric? He is a good person." I stopped speaking to God for a little while until Mama checked me and reminded me that God was still in control. Eric had two major surgeries and months of physical therapy. Both stab wounds were serious and could have been fatal. I had to do some counseling myself because I was messed up. I blame myself for what happened. I also blame Jonathan's sorry ass. With the loss of Jonathan's father and too much alone time, I believed he snapped. But I thank God Eric survived with the best doctors, the support of our families, the church and plenty of prayers.

My youngest sister Tiffany continues to amaze me as the youngest art director for a national prestigious art gallery here in Georgia. She travels the world looking for the most unique art. She also initiated the special events gala which now brings in nice lucrative amounts of money monthly for the gallery. Since she's been the director of the gallery, she has been in several well-known magazines. Tiffany has been awarded "Top Businesswomen" two years in a row now. As far as her dating life, she takes that slow especially after the disaster with Tony who tried to literally kill us and still our land that's been in the family for decades. Who does that shit?! But we took care of that little problem and we don't speak about it at all. Tiffany has been dating a young lady for a while but keeps tellin' us it isn't serious. I think she's tryin' to convince herself it's not that serious. She's just keeping up her guard after being used by Tony. Beware of Tiff, she is a devout Christian. What do I mean by that? She loves church and knows the Bible like the back of her hand. If you come for her, she doesn't believe in turning the other cheek. She's the big ass Pitbull that will snap your neck and pray later for forgiveness. I just want her to be sincerely happy. I guess that will come in time and that's why she spends so much time working at the gallery.

Leah, my middle sister has been working hard to finish her master's degree which she will present to Mama and Daddy as a surprise. When Leah abruptly dropped out of Spelman her freshman year, we all were disappointed. I was devastated because I was partly responsible. If only I had stayed with her at that party. Leah is the kind and trusting sister, too trusting sometimes. I tried to fix everything, but it wasn't enough. It tore our relationship apart for a while, but it seemed like forever. Time was the only thing that could heal our relationship along with a lot of praying. Leah decided to join the Army to study computers and finish school. Not only did she get her bachelor's degree but now she just finished her master's degree. Leah was studying day and night. When she wasn't studying, she was working. None of us hardly saw her anymore. But her hard work paid off. So, we're having a celebration that is a long overdue and family get-together as well. She even talked about pledging Delta Sigma Theta graduate chapter. Crimson and cream run through our family's blood among other things. She told Mama and Daddy she got a promotion and we're having a celebration at her place. Her boyfriend Carlos, the Latin lover, as we like to tease and call him, is already in town. They have been on and off again for a couple of years. But this time I think they're gonna make it.

Finally, there's Teresa, our newest and oldest sister. That sounds crazy to say, "Newest and Oldest sister." I have been the oldest and the protector of the three of us but now there are four. An unspeakable act happened to Mama a few years before I was born and out of that tragedy Teresa was born. Mama placed her up for adoption so Teresa could have a clean slate without the negative stigmatism from the town gossip to follow her for the rest of her life. Unfortunately, Teresa who also has our gifts, grew up with anger in her heart because she felt Mama didn't come for her as a child. As time went by, Teresa became very bitter. Teresa set out on this plan of vengeance to expose Mama and her dirty little secret. But when Teresa confronted Mama, and my sisters, they all found out about

*Blood, Secrets and Lies 2 The Grave*

the rape. No one was expecting to hear that. I believe the ice that surrounded Teresa's heart suddenly melted and shame set in because Mama didn't hear from Teresa for a while. It took a while for all of them to come to grips with what happened to Mama. Over time I saw Teresa go from this angry scheming bitch, to a quiet humble person. Maybe she was embarrassed by the way she initially approached us or maybe some good old-fashioned counseling helped. Do I trust her completely or call her my sister? Not yet. But most importantly she had let the anger towards Mama go. Mama and Teresa have a nice relationship. Leah is close to Teresa also. Surprisingly, Tiffany is okay with her seeing how Tiffany put a broken glass bottle to Teresa's neck demanding why she was at our home uninvited. I still have to check in with Tiffany just to make sure she's not talkin' about killin' Teresa slowly.

I was like an excited kid waiting to go to Leah's so-called promotion party. I called a few days before asking what she needed me to bring to the pitch-in. She said she was fryin' some chicken and fish so whatever side dishes I wanted to make was fine with her. Leah was bringing the drinks and Mama was making a caramel cake, peach cobbler and a sweet potato pie which happened to be all our favorites. She told Teresa to bring some wine. Before I hung up Tiffany said, "Hey Ree can you also bring a photocopy of the seven sisters? I can't seem to find mine. I seem to have misplaced it in one of the boxes when I moved here." I told her I would make a copy and frame it for her. Wow. It's been a while since anyone has mentioned the seven sisters or the, "Keepers of the light" as they are also known as. Great-grandma Emma who was Mama's grandmother on her mom's side of the family passed down a family photo album to my grandmother who we called, Gram-T. Gram-T then passed it down to Mama and us. It was a large photo album filled with thick black faded pages that will cut the tips of your fingers off if you weren't careful. Each black and white photo was encased with dingy white protective corners. On the first page, there is a photo of seven sisters. They were born around the 1840s. They live in a small village south of Johannesburg, South Africa. Their village was rated by savages, killing most of the elders, taking all resources and raping the young ladies while burning the entire village. The sisters fled to the deepest part of the jungle hoping to return later to rebuild and reunite with their family. After days of wandering in the jungle, the sisters found refuge in a big dark secluded cave that was covered with branches and vines. They had to learn to survive, eating roots, herbs, berries and whatever they could catch. In the middle of the night, the oldest sister was on watch and notice further back in the cave, a bright light. She discovered a large purple stone about the size of a baseball. The stone looks like a rock made from glass. She stooped down to pick it up. Her hand was cut deep. Blood spilled out as though she was cut by sharp blade. As she yelled in agony, her sisters awoke to find her standing there holding this rock while blood was running from her hand. Suddenly she passed out. They tried everything to revive her. Her body was on fire. No herbs or any roots were helping. Finally, after a few hours, she regained consciousness feeling no pain and her wound was completely healed. She felt good. She described to her sisters that she had this renewed strength. Her eyes had a strange yellow glow of fire inside them. The limp she had all her life was gone. She went outside to bathe in the river. All the scars on her body were all healed completely. Her thin hair was now thick. She said she had knowledge about things she never knew. She could see the past as well as know the outcome of the future. She told her sisters, they needed to experience the same thing. So, the sisters did a ritual of cutting their hands with the purple rock while they stood under the stars at night. The older sister wrapped the sister's hair up with a white cloth and poured water down their faces as a cleansing ritual. As they gathered in a circle holding hands, they began to pray. As they began to pray, the blood that dripped down their hands had completely disappeared. They gave thanks for their blessings and prayed for guidance. They all had renewed strength and spirit. They all had different gifts. They made a promise to use the gifts to provide, praise and protect. In order to continue to survive, they all learn how to, fish, plant, and study different herbs and roots. Most importantly they needed to know how to fight. They trained daily. Their fighting was different from what we call fighting today. When fire filled their eyes and the purple rock glowed, trees were set on fire, the winds blew with intensity and the rain came down like a tsunami. A single look from them could change your thoughts but a single touch could stop your heart.

They decided it was time to go back to their village after two years in the jungle. When they return, they only found remains of huts and tents. Most of the people that survived left the village. Some stayed and try to rebuild but it wasn't the same because of the miners. South Africa became the home of the two largest gold mines in the world.

There were always scavengers looking for gold and diamonds. One night while the village was quiet, the sisters heard horses approaching from miles away. Instead of alerting the village, they took it upon themselves to take care of the trespassers. They hid behind the trees waiting. There were three men on horses demanding gold found in the mines. One man jumped off his horse with an intense look and said, "I ain't ever seen a brown beauty like this." The men were told to leave. They just laughed as the other two dismounted their horses. One man noticed the purple glow coming from one of the sister's sacks and demanded to see it. He pulled out a machete walking towards her. She began to chant:

*"There are three lights that burn bright*
*the sun and the moon which is out tonight*
*but fire is the brightest of all the lights*
*may it touch your soul without a fight."*

The wind blew hard. The man suddenly stopped in his tracks out of fear. All the sisters began to chant. Suddenly all three men fell to the ground grasping for air while their eyes rolled in the back of their heads. Their skin began to smoke and turn beet red. The men felt the fire burning from within. Their flesh was completely black like charcoal. The youngest sister brought the rain down to wash away the remains. The sisters returned to the village. They all agreed that everyone needed to leave. It would never be safe again. They knew they couldn't carry the purple stone without getting unwanted attention from the glow. What better way to hide the stone, than to break it up and place it in a necklace, bracelet or even a ring. It would hide in plain sight. This is how I got my ring with the purple stone; Leah has a bracelet and Tiffany has a necklace. We are the descendants of the "Keepers of the light." We have history right in our hands. We still have some of the original scrolls, scrapbooks and worn cloaks. But out of all of keepsakes, my favorite is the photo. It captures the beauty of my ancestors. So, when I am questioned or even challenged as to who I am, I am reminded in this photo, of who we are and where we came from.

I ran a few errands, getting a photocopy of the seven sisters, a custom frame and a gift card to the spa. Tiffany was having yellow roses, which was Leah's favorite, delivered to her place. She'll be so surprised. She deserves this and so much more. On my way home from the store, I picked up sandwiches for dinner. Eric was still at the gym. Since his recovery from the awful stabbing, he works out five days a week. I still worry that he's overdoing it. To see him lying there in the hospital bed hooked up to machines not knowing his fate really tested my faith. This was the time when I thought God wasn't listening to me because I almost took matters into my own hands. I felt like Eric's condition was my fault. I had to fix it. On my way to the police station, I thought of every way to hurt Jonathan for stabbing Eric on our wedding day. I worked out a plan to get back to see Jonathan in jail. I planned to give him a slow death. Even though Mama tried to talk me out of it, I just couldn't rest until I spit in Jonathan's face. I arrived at the police station to find Mama standing by her car in the parking lot with a look of disappointment on her face. Shit! Needless to say, she stopped me from making a terrible mistake that I would have regretted or maybe not.

The next day, the hair salon was busy. I was working from sunup to sundown. Kim, my other stylist, and I were doing hair like it was the Bronner Brothers hair show again. I guess kids were going back to school, job interviews or ladies just wanting to look fabulous for no reason because we stayed busy. Each night I got home, I crawled in the bed next to Eric. I was so tired my skin hurt. Eric suggested I cut back on my hours. There was no need to work these crazy hours. I told him I was saving money for a rainy day. Whatever that meant. I was thinking about hiring another stylist to work my chair while I just manage both salons. We talked about having kids, but we had to put those plans on hold for a while or at least until the doctor gave us the green light. We got the green light, but I didn't want to rush Eric until I felt he was ready physically and emotionally. He would always tell me, "Hell yeah I'm ready! We can start now if you take off your panties!" I told him we can start tomorrow. I was too tired, and I needed to get up early in the morning before I go to work to cook for Leah's party tomorrow night.

I made a seven-layer salad and a pot of spaghetti. I put both in the refrigerator so when I'm done at work, all I need to do is change clothes and head out. When I got to work there was a client I didn't know with a child. She asked if I did walk-ins and if I did children's hair. I told her I did walk-ins but not children. Kids can be temperamental. They don't sit still long and sometimes no down-home trainin'. She told me her stylist had an emergency and had to cancel. Her daughter had school pictures today. She said she would pay anything. I told her I'll help her out, but we don't style kids. She was grateful. I started washing the child's hair. Her mom said she needed to go down the street to get some bows for her hair. Kim gave me a crazy look. She knew I didn't want to be babysittin' anybody's kid. Next thing I know this mother left and the kid starts telling me how to do her hair. This little girl had the nerve to ask for extra hair to be added in. Kim busted out laughin'. I finally told the little girl that she'll take whatever style I give her, or she'll leave out of here like her hair was caught on fire. She was very quiet after that. The rest of the day was slow.

When Eric and I got to Leah's place, everyone was already there. Leah and Mama were fryin' chicken and fish. Daddy and Carlos were watching a game. Tiffany was setting the table. Teresa was making lemonade. We were all ready to eat so Leah could present her surprise to Daddy and Mama. Daddy blesses the food and we all dug in. Eric piled his plate high and so did I. Just because I'm a lady doesn't mean I have to eat light. I can throw down with the best and not look like it, or at least at this age. As I was cutting the cake, Leah said she wanted me to get everyone in the living room so we could give Mama and Daddy their gifts.

Tiffany came into the kitchen and said, "Everyone is already in the living room. Let's go. Hurry up. I got my camera ready although Daddy been takin' pictures since he got here."

I turned off the TV and said, "I just want to say how proud I am of Leah and all of her hard work to get this promotion one her job."

Tiffany jumped up and said, "So does that mean Leah is takin' us on a paid vacation?"

Just then, Leah comes out of the room with two wrapped boxes and handed each one to Mama and Daddy. They both had a puzzled look on their face.

Mama said, "What's this? It's not our anniversary. We bought you a gift in honor of your promotion."

Daddy opened his box and saw a bachelor's degree with Leah's name on it. He held it up for everyone to see. Mama couldn't believe it. She rushed to open her box to find a master's degree. She didn't say a word. She just hugged Leah as tears flowed down.

Leah said, "I know when I suddenly dropped out of Spelman College and joined the service, that's not what you had planned for me or what I had planned for myself. But God has a way of working things out for our good. I also had to work out some things myself."

Mama said, "So you didn't get a promotion?"

Leah responded, "No. This is about celebrating you and Daddy. After I told you I was dropping out of school, you both still supported me. You also told me I wasn't gonna just sit around and do nothing. You told me I needed to come up with a plan B. An idea. It took a while to complete, but I did it with the support of all of you. Thanks, everyone. Now let's have some cake before I start to cry."

"Congratulations Leah," said Teresa.

Tiffany said, "So does this mean we ain't getting' a paid vacation from Leah?"

We all laughed while Mama whispered in my ear, "Did you know about this?"

I whispered, "Does it matter?"

Mama said, "I told you she would find her way."

# Chapter Two

# Who Did It?

Tiffany called me early Monday morning to tell me more about the troubles she was having at the art gallery with her new regional director. She said everything Tiffany did, she had to find something wrong. She even made the comment about Tiffany being too young to be the director of the art gallery despite all her accomplishments. Because of Tiffany's innovative ideas and marketing strategies, the art gallery has had more events each month, like the mayor's ball, weddings and company parties than it had in the past years. Tiffany has been working there since her freshman year in college on the weekends, during the summers till now.

Tiffany said, "You know Ree the bitch is a straight out racist. She has a hard time seeing me, a young black educated woman in a director's position. It's a shame in this time that I still have to deal with this shit. Ree, you know being one of the dark skin black little girls in school was always an ongoing fight. To be called, "black dog or monkey" in elementary by who I thought were my friends, these white girls, were eye-opening. Going to the store to get a baby doll and the salesperson tells you we don't have a doll that looks like you while a little white girl laughed, hurt me. That's why I was always angry. It's not easy being the dark sistah in the family. But I thank God for the people in our family who always told me and all of us that we are beautiful just the way God made us. I'll never forget one Louisiana summer at Gram- T's house, and I was in a store with Uncle Mac. This little white boy around my age asked if he could touch my hair. Uncle Mac went off on him. I didn't understand why the boy wanted to touch my hair and why Uncle Mac was so upset. Uncle Mac told him, "Hell Naw! Git the hell on!" The little boy's mom came over and dragged him out of the store embarrassed. He later explained that little boy not knowing, wasn't used to seeing little girls looking like me, girls of color. And on top of that a dark complexion little girl. My hair wasn't like the little white girls and my skin complexion wasn't like

*Blood, Secrets and Lies 2 The Grave*

theirs either. He told me God made us all different and some folks are just used to their own little world. But the most important thing he said was, "No matter what you are called or what they think they see, you know who you are. You are a beautiful black beauty. They may fear you or be intimidated by you but that's their problem. You are a beautiful black beauty who is powerful and will do great things. You girls always remember that." So, when I meet these racist mothafuckas they fear me because I know who I am."

I asked her what she planned to do about this woman. "I hope you're not planning on killing her."

Tiffany snapped back, "Why do y'all always think I'm gonna kill somebody?!

"Shit, cause that's usually your first response to people who piss you off." We both laugh. I suggested keeping records for a history of her negative behavior and filing a complaint with the higher-ups. There's nothing worse than having a great job that you love but with an awful boss. We both went to bed.

I was planning a romantic evening. Eric and I were working long hours. All we do is eat and sleep.

I must admit, I'm still a little timid about sex even though he's been out of therapy for a while. We have sex but I'm always asking, "You okay? Does that hurt?" I know it probably gets on his nerves but the last thing I want is for him to have a heart attack while we're going strong or worse. I call the EMTs, and they come in to see him layin' there with a big ol' rock hard dick going to waste while he's in pain. I know that sounds crazy when you say it out loud. Even I had to laugh. I just want my husband to be completely okay. So that's why I'm putting together a romantic evening. I bought a sexy nurse costume just for the occasion. I'm cooking steak, potatoes, with fresh green beans and my honeypot will be dessert.

I called Eric to see what time he will be home for dinner. I told him not to go to the gym tonight and come straight home. He asked if we had plans for tonight that he forgot about. I just told him I have plans for him. We both laugh. Just as I finished cooking and on my way to the shower, the phone rang. It was Leah calling to say thank you for helping with the family get together and the gift card. I rushed her off the phone because I wanted to get ready for Eric who will be home in 30 minutes. I want to take a deep cleansing shower, meaning I want every crack and crevice clean because I like to be licked from head to toe if you know what I mean. I put on my see-through lace blacktop with my satin push-up bra. Trust me when I say my girls were sittin' up high. I had on Eric's favorite cutup jeans. I made a few extra cuts right under my butt cheeks. By the time I lit all of the candles in the house, Eric was walking through the door. He had to take a second look before getting into the shower. The food was delicious. He even went back for seconds. He asked what was for dessert. I gave him a devilish look while spreading my legs wide. I told him, "Sweetheart I need you to wait right here." There was a chair in the middle of the living room that I had placed earlier. I ran back in the bedroom to change into my white see-through bra with the nipples exposed, matching thong and white nurse's hat. I slowly strutted in my 6-inch clear high-heeled shoes with a stethoscope wrapped around my neck into the living room while music played in the background. I turned off the lights. I slowly took off his clothes and poured him a glass of champagne that he gulped down in one swallow. I swayed back and forth slowly while pouring honey down my breasts as I removed my bra. I turned around bending over with my ass in his face wiggling my plump cheeks. He leaned over and kissed each cheek, but I turned back around and motioned, "No" like a teacher disciplining her student. I gently tied his hands behind him. I slowly leaned over in front of him just close enough so my big brown nipples would just slightly brush up against his full lips. I backed up and removed my thong as I lay on my back on the floor. I poured more honey between my breasts and slowly drippin' some between my thighs as it slowly drizzled into my honeypot with my legs wide open. I began to touch myself all over while licking each finger. As honey dripped from my mouth, I began to crawl to Eric slowly. Eric's eyes grew bigger and bigger and so did his dick.

I asked, "How many licks does it take to get to the center of the lollipop?" I began lickin', suckin', and strokin' until he was at full attention. Before he could explode, I pulled back. I slowly laid back on the floor with my legs spread wide open like a V.

I heard him say, "Ah shit." I drizzled more honey between my legs while turning over and backing my ass in his face. He broke loose and caressed my cheeks. I felt his long-wet tongue go up and down my crack. With one hand he turned me over. His mouth was eating every inch of my goodness. I was on fire. Before I could explode, he slowly kissed

*Blood, Secrets and Lies 2 The Grave*

my breasts while gently biting my nipples just the way I love it. I put my tongue down his throat gently tasting the honey. I opened my legs wide as he climbed in deep and hard. With every thrust, I moaned. I pushed him off and laid him down on his back. With a mouthful of ice, I made the joystick disappear once again. He yelled my name over and over. I mounted him like a wild stallion. He palmed my breasts and held on for the ride. I pulled him close to me as we both exploded. I could feel his heart beating.

He caressed my face while kissing me and said," I love you Ree."

I replied, "Hell Yeah! I know you do. Can't nobody give it to you the way I do?" We both jumped up in the shower. He was already in bed when I came back with a big bowl of ice cream.

He asked, "Is that to eat or is that for EAT-ING?" I handed him his spoon as I smiled.

Tiffany called and said a detective came to the gallery asking about Tony her ex-girlfriend. We hadn't talked about Tony since we took care of her a couple of years ago. We didn't kill her although Tiffany tried. The last detectives came to see Tiffany when we got back from Louisiana where we left

Tony alive. Can you imagine dating someone just to get even for your family's sake? That's absolutely crazy! Now Tony's sister who Tiffany never met has been talking to the detectives recently. Some dead girl's remains have been found and Tony's sister thinks the remains are Tony's. Tiffany is now the number one suspect because they dated, and Tiffany was the last to see her. I reminded Tiffany that we didn't have anything to worry about because we left Tony alive in Louisiana. Long story short, we had a family get together in Louisiana a couple of years ago. Tiffany invited Tony to meet the family. Tony had plans of her own without anyone knowing. Tony was a part of the Johnson family, which is a rival family that has been feuding with our family since Gram-T was a kid. She tried to poison my family in hopes to get Mama to sign over our family land that she thought was stolen from her great-grandfather and leave us for dead. Needless to say, she failed. We wiped her memory away and my uncles dropped her ass off in the Canal Square and we never look back. Now some estranged sister, named Sherry is desperate to find Tony and the police are trying to put this shit on Tiffany. Oh Hell Naw! According to the coroner's office, the remains are the same age, size, and gender as Tony. The detective said they are waiting to

*Blood, Secrets and Lies 2 The Grave*

confirm dental records if Tony had any. The body was buried in a shallow grave in the cemetery. We know damn well we didn't do that! I asked Tiffany why they think that was Tony's body.

She said, "They said they found a bracelet or somethin' that I gave to Tony on top of the grave."

I said, "What the hell! That some sick shit that deranged killers do when they want to get caught."

Tiffany said, "They are looking back at everyone from Tony's past. I told them the same thing I told them a couple of years ago, that Tony and I got into an argument in Louisiana. Tony said she was leaving me for somebody else. We parted ways. I got my belongings from her place while she wasn't there, and we haven't spoken since."

I asked, "Has Tony's sister ever confronted you?"

Tiffany said, "Naw, never met the girl."

"We may need to take a trip to New Orleans to find Tony." I said

Tiffany replied, "Or maybe I need to go meet Tony's sister first. We could call Uncle Mac and Uncle Joe and have them go to Canal Square to see if she's still there. Either way, they ain't puttin' this death on me!"

That night after Eric went to bed, I called Mama and told her about the detectives visiting Tiffany. She said she would call Uncle Mac and Uncle Joe and have them check Canal Square and Bourbon Street where a lot of the homeless stay. Mom was concerned that Tiffany would take matters into her own hands. I reassured Mama that Tiffany was fine for the moment. But Tiffany was adamant about not taking a murder charge for this Jane Doe. Mama said she will call one of the deacons from church who was an attorney to get some advice.  She also said Tiffany should stop speaking to the detectives unless they have a warrant with her name on it.

I was thinkin' what I could do in the meantime. Tiffany no longer had any of Tony's belongings except her family photo album. If she had a piece of hair, jewelry or clothing I could do a spell to see if she is still alive. Maybe a photo from her album would work to do a spell. But I need to check with Tiffany first to see if she was okay with it. I tend to overstep when it comes to my family. I still wouldn't mind goin' to New Orleans either. This also gives us a chance to see our family. Eric's

*Blood, Secrets and Lies 2 The Grave*

family is from Indiana. I'll plan to go to Louisiana next week while Eric's out of town.

Like clockwork, Leah called. She just got off the phone with Tiffany. Leah asked if I had a plan.

I told her, "You know I do. I think we need to go to New Orleans and get proof that Tony is still alive. Because every dead Jane Doe that pops up will be Tony according to her sister. Or I could do another mind sweep and clear the sister's memory and be done with all of this shit."

Leah said, "Ree you know doing a mind sweep is dangerous. We don't know what happened to Tony if she's dead or alive. I say we wait on the dental work for the Jane Doe to show that she's not Tony. Then we go to New Orleans to find Tony."

I agreed reluctantly. I'm so sick of shit with the Johnson family.

Before the end of the week came, the same detective came to Tiffany's place asking if she could come to the station for more questions. Tiffany said she would meet the detective at the station with her attorney present and her family. He didn't have a warrant. He assumed since Tiffany was an open book the last time they spoke, she would speak freely again. To his surprise he was wrong.

I picked Mama and Tiffany up. Attorney Smith met us at the police station. The attorney advised Mama and I to keep quiet. He told Tiffany to keep her answers short and simple and to look in his direction to get the okay to answer each question. They asked the same questions, "How long Tiffany and Tony dated, any big fights, was anyone cheating?"

Of course, Tiffany's patience wore thin and said, "I've answered all of these questions before, don't you have a copy?! My answers haven't changed!"

"Is there something new in the case?" Attorney Smith asked.

The detective pulled out a plastic bag with a necklace in it. It was a silver Yen and Yang charm on a black string. I could tell Tiffany recognized it.

Attorney Smith asked, "So what's this?"

The detective said it was found on top of the grave where the body was found.

"Do you recognize it, Tiffany?" The detective said.

Before Tiffany could answer, the attorney said, "Wait, Tiffany, even if it was my client's necklace, why would she leave it to be found if she was guilty? Anyone could have put it there. Have you checked for fingerprints or DNA? Everyone in their mama has that necklace or a tattoo of it. Hell my son has a tattoo of it on his arm. Tiffany wasn't the only one Tony was seeing. That should be in your records. She told you that already. If that's all you got, we'll be going now."

We all got up. As we were leaving, this lady approached us. We didn't recognize her.

She demanded, "I know you had somethin' to do with my sistah Tony's death. As soon as the coroner's report comes back, yo ass is goin' to jail. I see you girl!"

"Bitch I didn't kill your sister! She left me! I moved on!" Tiffany yelled back.

Attorney Smith said, "Don't say anything else, let's go."

The woman yelled, "I got somethin' for you."

I looked at her and said calmly, "Are you threatenin' my sister? Naw, you don't wanna do that."

"Ree let's go." Mama said.

The lady appeared to be slow in a mental way. She kept sayin' the same thing over and over till we left.

We went to Tiffany's place, to make sure she was okay. We all were upset because we knew whoever this poor lady they found in the grave, wasn't Tony. We left Tony in Louisiana. But I was thinkin', what if the mind sweep didn't work, what if she found her way back home? Who would let their family believe they were dead? Somethin' is not adding up. I went to the car to get Tony's old family photo album that we took when Tiffany and I went to her apartment to get the rest of her stuff. She left Tony's key and her necklace along with all of the other trinkets Tony gave her on the table. I told her to leave all that shit. We all looked through the photos. We saw Tony and her younger brother who died at a young age. The third girl who we assumed was Tony's sister, didn't look like the lady who was threatening us at the police station. There were other girls in the photo album of different ages, but none resembled this lady. She seems older than us. Somethin' isn't right. I asked Mama if we could do a revealing spell using a photo of Tony? It would tell us whether Tony was

*Blood, Secrets and Lies 2 The Grave*

alive and maybe we wouldn't have to take a trip to New Orleans. Mama went through the cabinets to get mugwort, acacia, honeysuckle, and peppermint herbs and spices. At a young age, we all were taught to keep herbs and roots for occasions such as this. Tiffany used an old photo of Tony with two other kids in the background. Mama laid the roots in the pot and burned them until they became ashes. We removed our family stones from our jewelry and place them in the pot as well. Next, the photo was placed on top of the stones.

Mama said these words as the stones began to glow,

**"Seek is to find in this late hour of time,**

**Reveal to us all if the Angel of Death has called."**

Suddenly the corners of the picture went up in flames. All that was left was Tony's silhouette. Mama said the silhouette of Tony means she's still alive. The other two girls are dead.

Mama said, "So now we know that's not Tony in the grave and she is still alive. So who was that in the grave and why are they blaming Tiffany? Well, that's for the detectives to find out and not us. It's probably some poor runaway or homeless girl. We need to pray for her soul and her family. Ree, I mean it. Let the police do their jobs. Until then, I'll call Mac and Joe to see if they've seen Tony in the Square."

The next couple of days, we were all on pins and needles. It was hard to act like nothin' happened around Eric when I was worried about my family. The next few days seem to drag. Finally, Tiffany called and said she spoke with Attorney Smith. He told Tiffany that the Jane Doe wasn't Tony but a person with similar DNA meaning a relative. But who killed her and why would they try to put this murder on Tiffany? This is absolutely crazy! It's probably those damn Johnsons. I'm worried about Tiffany. Tiffany isn't the one you want to push. Leah on the other hand, is the sensible one. I'm the calm one but I'll hurt someone if I need to. Tiffany will hurt you too and hurt you badly if she feels you have backed her in a corner. So I keep checking on her to make sure she remains calm and hasn't hurt anyone.

Leah called to see what I decided to do even though Mama said to let the police handle it. It's hard for me to be still. I told her Tiffany and I thought about goin' to the country morgue. According to the local news, the body was still being examined. Low and behold, Tony's sister was on the news ranting, "I know who did this and she knows too!" She just kept repeating the same thing even though news reporter kept asking for a name.

Leah said, "Ree, I know you and Tiffany aren't just goin' to walk into the morgue lookin' for this body, do a spell and walk out like no big deal? You guys could get into a lot of trouble if you get caught."

I said, "I'm just goin' to get some of her hair, maybe a piece of clothing and get the hell out of there. We could use a third person to be the lookout or distraction for us to get back where the bodies are. We don't plan to be there long. There are three entrances to the place. I went by there yesterday. One entrance in the front, on the side where the hearse parks and one in the rear. It seems the side door is always open."

"Wait, you mean to tell me that you already scoped out the place and came up with a plan?! Ree are you crazy?!" Leah demanded.

I told her she can pretend to be a family member that was bringing close for her deceased cousin while Tiffany and I sneak in through the side door. Once again, she told me I was crazy, and I was obsessed with this dead lady. I told her I'm not obsessed with the dead woman but makin' sure Tiffany's name is completely clear and makin' sure Tony isn't skulkin' around here. We may need to take a girl's trip to Louisiana. At least that's what we can tell the fellas.

Leah said, "So I guess Tiffany is all on board with your plan?"

I said, "You know she is. Just think about it Leah, please. We're not hurting anybody. She's already dead. We'll be in and out. You have to admit somethin' is wrong. This lady is a Johnson and her sister thinks Tiffany killed her. We know Tiffany didn't do it. But the slow sister thinks so. I'm thinkin', we may have to pay her a visit too."

Leah said, "Slow down Ree. You doin' too much. You talkin' about going into a morgue lookin' for a dead body. She won't be layin' there with a neon sign with her name on it. You will have to look at other bodies while tryin' to find her. You don't know what she looks like. Can you even handle looking at dead bodies? Not all of the bodies will be intact. Can you stomach a decomposed body? You have no idea the condition of her body."

Oh my goodness. I totally had to calm Leah down. I'm sure there are nametags with each of the bodies. I hope. The last thing I want to do is going through a bunch of dead bodies and tryin' to explain to Eric the terrible smell on me. Leah asked me, when do Tiffany and I plan to go through this crazy plan. I told her tonight.

She yelled, "What?! Girl are you crazy?!"

I told her, "Leah they don't hold dead bodies for long. So time isn't on our side. So are you comin' with us or not? We need your help. You can just take a dress to the front desk as a distraction while Tiffany and I looked through the bodies."

Leah took a deep breath and said, "Okay. Somebody needs to keep you guys out of jail."

I told Eric I would probably get home late tonight so don't wait up. I picked Leah up first then Tiffany. When Tiffany came outside, we both laugh. Tiffany was dressed in black hiking boots, black jeans, and a black shirt. To top it off, she had black leather gloves with a black ski mask. She looked like something from a spy movie. She was carrying two dresses she got from a thrift store. We got to the morgue there were two cars outside in the front. We parked down the street and walked behind the building. Leah went around the front. Tiffany and I went to the side door. It was locked.

So we had to go around to the back. The main hallway had two gurneys outside with bodies. I was nervous as hell. They both had toe tags, so we didn't have to lift up the sheets because they were men. We came to a door with a glass window. Tiffany slowly peeked in and said there were three bodies. Then we heard a car pull up. We tiptoed inside the room and close the door quietly while looking outside the window. It was the hearse pulling up to unload another body. I almost pissed myself. We both ran into the small office next to the room we were in. There was a tiny bathroom that we snuck into. I thought I was going to throw up not because of the smell of the bodies, but someone just took a big ass dump. I put my hand over Tiffany's mouth before she could say somethin'. I cracked the door to find two men delivering another body while the coroner signed a clipboard. He told them to leave the body in the hallway. He also laughed and said that there was a crazy hysterical girl up front trying to drop off some clothes for a dead relative, but I'm trying to tell her she needs to take them close to the funeral home. He even said she was cute as they all laughed. Then he said the crazy girl started crying. I was thinkin', "You go Leah." The coroner finally said he had to go and get rid of her. We had to move quickly. I unzipped the first bag, and it was an elderly woman. Tiffany unzipped the second bag and it turned out to be another man. The third bag was very small. Tiffany went to unzip it, but I stopped her. I told her it probably was a child. We didn't need to see that. We slowly pulled out the metal drawers. They all had toe tags. The third body was labeled Jane Doe. I took a deep breath. I gently pulled some strands of her hair and placed them in a Ziploc bag. I glanced down at her face just for a moment wondering who could be so cruel. She favored the little girl that was in Tony's picture that we burned. She had the same birthmark, a big black mold on the side of her nose about the size of the dime that the little girl had in the picture. Tiffany wanted to take a picture of her. I told her quietly, "No. We don't take pictures of the dead. Plus, we don't want any evidence that we were here."

Tiffany whispered, "She ain't in our family."

We snuck out the back door and met Leah down the street.

We went back to Tiffany's place. I grabbed Tony's photo album. Tiffany grabbed a pot with some roots and herbs. We looked through the album and found several pictures of Tony in the same little girl with the big mole on her nose like this woman.

We burned the roots and herbs until they turned into ashes. Then placed the photo on top. We each removed our purple stones and place them in the pot. I placed a couple of hair strands, saving some for later, from the dead woman in the pot. Tiffany did a chant. As she recited the chant the photo split into two pieces. As our stones began to glow, the side of the picture with the little girl with the mole on her nose slowly burned into ashes with red smoke covering it. The silhouette of Tony remained untouched. This meant the woman in the morgue, was the little girl in the picture who happens to be Tony's sister or her cousin. The red smoke means blood was spilled, meaning murder.

Tiffany said, "Shit! If that's Tony's sister or cousin in the morgue, then who in the hell is the crazy lady?! Is she really one of the sisters? We got a crazy nut as a killer running around town. We need to tell Mama and the family so they can be on guard.

We called Mama and put her on speaker phone. That wasn't a pleasant conversation. She yelled at all of us for a good ten minutes about not listening and letting the police do their jobs. Of course, she really yelled when she asked how we got the strands of hair. The three of us just sat

*Blood, Secrets and Lies 2 The Grave*

there like little girls. I remember when Tiffany first came into her gifts at thirteen. Mama took all three of us out late night to a park to practice our spells and chants. We were always told not to mix spells together, but Tiffany being Tiffany and Leah encouraging her did it anyway. We were learning the use of fire and Tiffany decided to do just what Mama told her not to do. Being silly playin' after conjuring up a small fire, Tiffany blew the wind into our direction along with the fire. No one was hurt but we had to lie to daddy about why none of us had any eyebrows and Tiffany had a burn mark on her nose. Mama made Tiffany and Leah go to school without eyebrows as punishment. I also remember seeing two figures in the dark with glowing eyes watching us. I was thinkin' great, now two other folks or some animals know we don't have eyebrows either. But this current situation is crazy. Mama said she would call Uncle Mac and Uncle Joe and tell them what was goin 'on. The three of us decided to do a protection spell.

Leah said these words,

**"As descendants of the keepers of the light, protect us each and every night**

**Be our eyes in the back of our head, show us our enemies that lie ahead."**

Tiffany asked, "So Leah, how did you keep the coroner upfront?"

Leah had a smirk on her face and said, "I played the slow grieving cuzin'. I told him in my southern backwoods drawl, I was bringin' my favorite cuzin' a dress to wear for the family viewing, funeral and repass. At first, he looked at me and asked If I was serious? I told him I was serious as a dog scootin' his ass across the fluffy carpet. He tried to interrupt me, but I kept talkin' about how my cuzin' was into fashion, so I know she needed several changes of clothes for her home goin'. Hell, I even held up the dresses to show him. I think he felt sorry for me. When I asked him, did the black shoes go with all three dresses, he nodded his head saying yes. He stopped me again and explained that I was in the wrong place to drop off clothes. He even suggested that I only needed one dress. He started walking to the door. I asked him if I could do her hair, a little wash and curl. Again he laughed and said I need to go to the funeral home. I really think he felt sorry for me because he began to tell me about his life story."

Tiffany said, "Girl, he didn't feel sorry for you. He was lovin' those tight ass jeans and titty tight shirt." We all laughed.

The next few days were busy at the salon. Eric said his sister who lives in Indiana, was giving her son a big birthday and invited us if we were available. I told him to go without me. But I was sending a gift. This gave me an excuse to do some more detective work. Somethin' about the way the crazy sister at the police station looked at me didn't sit well with me.

I stopped by the second salon to check on everyone. I try to do an appreciation lunch once a month. I have food catered on Fridays because that's one of our biggest moneymaker days. Everyone loves it. Happy and fed employees keep the drama down. I went home to help Eric pack. He was leaving tomorrow. And we all decided at the last minute, to go to Louisiana to hang out with family but also find Tony's ass. Mama planned to come to keep an eye on us and keep us from killin' anyone.

# Chapter Three

## Familiy Get Together

By the time we arrived in Louisiana at Uncle Joe's house, it was time to eat. You could smell the fried chicken from the porch. Everyone was there, Uncle Mac, his wife Aunt Bernice, their son Junior, Sandra, Phil, and their twins were all in the kitchen. Auntie, Mama's youngest sister and Sandra's mom, was pulling a poundcake out of the oven as we walked in. Sandra and I just hung out on the back porch like little kids once again. She has always been my sistah cuzin. I love her just as much as my sisters.

Uncle Joe yelled, "Alright, fall in line y'all know who does what. Sandra, Ree, y'all put the food on the table. Tiff get yo Gram-T's tablecloth and silverware. Junior gets a bag of ice out of the freezer from the shed. Leah can make the sweet tea. On second thought, the last time you put too much damn sugar in it. I thought my tooth was gonna crack. You can just get some bottles of water for the young folks and get some whiskey for the grown folks."

When the table was set, it looked like Gram-T's table during the holidays. Her beautiful lace tablecloth with her white China, made us all feel we were at a fancy five-star restaurant. My Grandpa Jerry carved the dining room table himself. It was somethin' to see. It had a beautiful mahogany finish. The table set sixteen people because Grandpa Jerry didn't believe in the kid's table. Some of the grown-ups may disagree including Uncle Joe and Uncle Mac. We had so much food to choose from. All of the favorites were on the table, fried chicken and gizzards, catfish, dirty rice, mac & cheese, black-eyed peas, greens with hot water cornbread and potato salad. Before I learned how to make cornbread from scratch like Gram-T, I use the box mix and try to pass it off as scratch cornbread. When Uncle Joe came to Georgia to visit and I made the box mix cornbread, he took one bite and said, "Who made this damn cornbread?" Everyone looked at me. He leaned over and whispered, "Ah Ree don't make this shit no more. I love you. Learn the family recipes." We all sat down to eat. Uncle

Joe blessed the food. I had a little of everything. Uncle Joe's wife, Auntie Pat, made peach cobbler, poundcake, and homemade ice cream just like Gram-T. Whether you are born into the family or married into the family, you have to know how to cook. Gram-T used to always tell us, food is not only essential for health, but it is essential to the heart. During our meals in Louisiana for the summer, it was a time of fellowship, a time to pray and lift each other up. It was also a time to share your thoughts, dreams, and a time of reflection. During one meal, I found out how my Grandpa Jerry's immediate family was murdered. But in that same meal, I also found out where some of our family's names came from. So having a meal isn't just about eating food. It's about our heritage, family and most importantly about giving God thanks. I had to unzip my jeans because I ate like a pig. Now my stomach was upset. I asked Uncle Joe if he had some Pepto-Bismol.

He replied, "Ree gone in the kitchen and get a teaspoon of baking soda and a glass of water. I don't know why you kids drink that pink stuff. It don't do nothin' but turns yo tongue black. You'll feel better. Don't forget we got to go take care of your business in the Quarters lookin' for yo girl Tony's ass."

I almost forgot the reason we were here. Everyone decided to head home. Auntie Pat went to sleep early. While Auntie Bernice said she would meet Uncle Mac at home. Mama and Auntie were in the kitchen burning herbs to provide a protection spell for us all. The plan was simple. Uncle Mac, Mama and Leah would look for Tony in one part of the Quarter. Uncle Joe, Junior, Tiffany and I would look in another area. If we found Tony, we would call the others. No one was supposed to put their hands on her, especially Tiffany. We were all still upset because of what Tony tried to do in the past. Tiffany showed everyone the only recent picture she could find of Tony. Tony was a beautiful brown skin curvy girl with beautiful long locks. She shouldn't be hard to find. I was really concerned about Tiffany and bringing up old feelings. Has Tiffany really gotten over Tony? I pulled Tiffany aside and suggested that she stay at the house.

Of course, she said, "Hell Naw! I didn't come all this way just to sit at the house and twiddle my thumbs. I got the right to look that bitch in her eyes. If she remembers me, I might give her an ass kickin' she'll never forget."

I asked, "What if she doesn't remember us? Are you willing to forgive her and walk away?"

Tiff looked me dead in my eyes and asked, "Have you forgiven Jonathan for stabbin' and tryin' to kill Eric?!"

I took a deep breath and said, "No because I tried to do the unthinkable to Jonathan and I provoked him." I held my head down in shame and tears in my eyes.

Tiff said, "What the hell are you talkin' about?! How in the hell could you have caused Jonathan to stab Eric?!"

I looked at her with one eyebrow raised.

She yelled, "Did you screw that mothafucka?!"

I quickly covered her mouth and told her to lower her voice. She asked me again. I didn't say a word. I just looked away. She turned my head back and asked, "Well?!"

Tiff said, "Oh my God, Ree, are you crazy?! Girrl, was the dick that good?! Shit it had to be. I can't believe it. You got Jonathan strung out. How have you been able to keep this to yourself?!"

I told her, "By not telling anyone. I want to keep it that way. We'll talk about this later. Right now we need to find Tony. Tiff please don't say a word. It has been killin' me not to say nothin'. Mama asked me at the hospital when Eric was stabbed if I had given Jonathan the wrong impression. I lied. It kills me to this day. And the worst of it all, Eric never even questioned me if I even slept with Jonathan. He trusted me and I betrayed him in the worst way."

Tiff said, "Ree I don't know what to say about that, but you might want to take that shit to the grave."

"Take what to the grave?" asked Mama as she walked into the kitchen lookin' at me.

I said, "Nothing. We're all ready to go."

Just as we arrived in the Quarters, it was starting to get dark. We had to move quickly. We split into our two groups. We combed through the streets like we were looking for a missing child. Could somebody please tell me where in the hell all of these homeless people get dogs? The smell of pee on the side streets made me want to throw up. It seemed like everyone had locks, braids or natural fros. We were having no luck. I saw this brown complexion lady singin' for money in a wheelchair. She could really sing. Her two front teeth were missin'. She had a long scar down the front of her leg. I have to wonder what her life story was. All of these people out here on the streets didn't choose to be here. Who wants to sleep outside on the ground with crazy extreme hot temperatures and never know if you'll eat another meal? The small things we take for granted, like bathing, using a clean toilet, having a family or friend just to talk with and clean clothes to put on. We looked in every joint, hole in the wall and restaurant. We called Mama a couple of times to check in. They hadn't seen Tony either. We were all getting hungry again. Uncle Joe called Uncle Mac and said to meet us at this place right around the corner called, "Black's." Apparently, this was someone that they all grew up with. He was supposed to have the best hot wings, gator bites, gumbo and fried green tomatoes in the South. But Uncle Joe also warned us of some of his shady dealings, like gambling, chop shop owner and had a small record company that he used as a front. Hell, I said never mind I'm not that hungry. Uncle Joe said we weren't going inside anyway. He'll just get the food and we'll wait in the van. Uncle Mac and Uncle Joe went in. We got out of the van to stretch our legs. About ten minutes later they came outside but were joined by a third man. He was tall, dark skin and had a ball head. I had to admit, he was fine for man his age. He wore a black leather jacket with black jeans and timberland boots. He had a smooth swag. Watching Uncle Mac, Uncle Joe and the mystery man walk out, looked like somethin' from an old gangsta movie. This man was smiling from ear to ear. He walked straight up to Mama and gave her a big hug as though he knew her in a special way.

Uncle Mac said, "Y'all this is Black." We all waved.

Black said, "It's good to see you, Shorty. It's been a long time. Too long. You look damn good."

Mama said, "How are you, Tim?"

He just smiled. Tiffany cleared her throat as though she was asking for an introduction.

Black turned around and said, "This must be Tiffany, Leah and Renee. Y'all want to come inside and have a drink?"

Tiffany said, "Naw we're good. We don't want our food to get cold."

Black replies, "Y'all can eat here. I'll make some drinks and my girl gonna sing some tunes. Y'all can stay a little while."

Mama looked at Uncle Mac and said, "We'll stay just for a little while."

They sat us at a large family table right in front of the stage. The band was already playin' jazz. It was a nice club. The food was actually good. I couldn't help but notice the way Mr. Black was lookin' at Mama. Mama was being nice but in a gentle polite kinda way. He asked how long we would be in town.

Leah responded, "Not long."

Black said, "I'm havin' a big cookout in the old park where we used to hang out as kids. We're just giving away hot dogs and hamburgers to the neighborhood kids and families. Like Rev. Edward used to do for us as kids. Rev. Edward loved y'all mama as he looked at Uncle Joe and Uncle Mac.

I asked, "Who was Rev. Edward?"

Black said, "He was the new preacher in town from Mississippi when we were kids. He wore fancy suits, big gold chains and gold rings."

Mama said, "Yeah and a big gold tooth in front of his mouth to match."

Black said, "All the ladies in the church were

chasin' after him. He said his wife died from some sickness. So he was a single father of a little girl lookin' for new mama for her. What pimp daddy wanted was… Ass. But when it came to Mrs. Thelma Sullivan, he couldn't step to her like some street cat. Yo grandfather didn't come to church at first when we were younger. Rev. Edward assumed Mrs. Sullivan was a widow. All the ladies knew he had eyes for her. But yo grandmother being a Christian woman was helping him with his daughter. She was pressing her hair every week. Rumors started flyin' around the church."

"Papa put an end to that shit quickly. Rev. Edward came to the family diner and asked to speak with Mama in the back. What Rev. Edward didn't know was, Papa was in the back doing inventory. Rev. Edward grabs mama's hand. Papa came out of nowhere and dragged Rev. Edward outside and beat the shit out of him. Needless to say, we found another church to go to. Later we all found out his wife wasn't dead. She was in a mental institution. He was going around robbin' churches and leaving town. He wasn't nothing but a con man." Uncle Mac said.

Black said, "I heard somebody caught up with that fool and put a bullet in his head. Anyway, y'all gonna stop by the park tomorrow before you head out? It's gonna be fun. We'll have food, singin' and dancin'."

Mama said, "I don't think so. But it was nice to see you Tim."

We all got up and left. On the way home, we all decided it probably was a good idea to go to the park tomorrow. There may be a chance that Tony would be there. We all went into the kitchen to have some more cobbler and ice cream. Uncle Joe went out on the back porch to smoke a cigar. I followed behind him.

I asked, "So who was Mr. Black to Mama?"

Uncle Joe smiled and said, "Maybe you should be askin' yo mama. It ain't no big deal. Black and his brother were kids we all grew up with. Black was a hell of a baseball player. Scouts were watchin' him in middle school. That fool was smart too. He was crazy about yo mama. She liked him too. They started datin'. One night he was over here hangin' out with all of us. His father came by and said Black's brother was jumped by a group of boys from another neighborhood and he was in the hospital. We all went to the hospital. Later that same night, Black's brother died from his injuries. Somethin' in

Black snapped. He didn't go to the funeral. Mama tried to check on him. He was never at home. Rumor was, he was lookin' for the fools who killed his brother. He started drinkin' and smokin'. He dropped out of school. The four mothafuckas who killed his brother mysteriously came up dead. One was stabbed, the other strangled, and the third was beaten with a baseball bat. The fourth left town. Black left town for a while as well. About two years later he came back. But he wasn't the same. Your mama moved on with her life but always hoped for the best for him. Black turned to the streets and has been there since. But at least he gives back to the community. He donates to the homeless, gives to the Boys and Girls Clubs, buys new equipment and baseball uniforms for all the Little League teams. He could have been one of the best baseball players in the league, but shit happens."

The next morning I called Eric to see how his visit with his sister was goin'. He said he was having a great time. I told him I'd be home in a few days. As we were all sittin' down for breakfast, I noticed Tiffany wasn't at the table. I went to the room and found her just staring outside the window with a blank look on her face.

I asked, "You okay?"

She said, "Yeah just wondering if we do find Tony, what's next? I still want to beat that bitch up. Maybe we can pin the murder of the Jane Doe on her and put all this shit to rest."

I just put my arm around her and told her to come and eat because she'll need her strength.

When we got to the park, surprisingly it was jam packed, music booming, and grilled hotdog aroma filled the air. There was even a huge stage set up for a band. Meanwhile, the DJ was playin'. The plan was to split into two groups and check back in at the stage every thirty minutes. The park was bigger than I remembered. First, we all stopped by Black's tent to say hello. It was like an exclusive VIP lounge with couches, big-screen TVs, and a cocktail bar. When he saw Mama, he dropped everything to greet her once more.

Black said, "Sup family? I'm glad y'all came out to support a brutha. We got plenty of food, whiskey and the band is about to play."

Mama said, "Tim you put all this together for the community?"

Black replied, "Yeah just a little somethin' to give back. You know I lost my Uncle Buck to the streets. Mac y'all gone and fix a plate and take a look around."

We split into our groups. It was me and Tiffany, Uncle Mac and Mama, Uncle Joe, and Leah, Junior and JJ, Uncle Joe's sons. We all went in different directions. There were so many people. Black even have portable bathrooms not just for peeing but for bathing for the homeless. I saw a lady with locks from behind, but I ran up to her thinking it was Tony. But it wasn't. Tiffany didn't say a word at all. She had a stern look on her face. I was scared if she saw Tony, she would hurt her. There were too many people out here to use our gifts without exposing ourselves. Mama called asking if we were okay. I told her we haven't seen Tony at all. But we kept moving. We all met at the stage after two hours had passed and we didn't see Tony. The band started setting up. The sun was going down. We knew we had to move quickly because it will be harder to find her in a crowd at night. Mama suggested getting some food and taking a break. We were able to get a picnic bench right in front of the stage. The band began to play. People all over started dancin'. We had to stay focused and remember why we were here.

Black came by and said, "Y'all gonna love this sistah I'm getting ready to bring to the stage. Sit tight."

Uncle Joe said, "We need to get moving again it's just about dark."

As we were discussing which areas to go in, Black grabbed the mic and said, "Y'all havin' a good time? Help me welcome this sistah to the stage. Our very own, Drew."

Everyone was going wild. Just as we started walkin' out in the crowd, our purple stones began to light up. Mama said, "Tony is close by."

Just as the young lady began singin' Tiffany stopped dead in her tracks and turned around. She didn't say a word.

I asked her, "Do you see Tony?"

Tiffany said, "She's right there." As she pointed to the stage.

"Right where?! I demanded. She pointed to the singer. Tiffany started walkin' back towards the stage. We all follow behind her.

Mama asked, "Tiff, Tim called her Drew not Tony."

"Drew is Tony's middle name. She's lost weight, not dressed so fancy anymore and her locks are cut." Tiffany said calmly. Fire filled Tiffany's eyes.

Uncle Mac said, "We can't just grab her off the stage. We'll have to wait till she's done."

I suggested that Tiffany walked past the front of the stage and see if Tony recognizes her. We may get a reaction from her and we'll know if she is still under the mind sweep. It was like Tiffany was walking a runway in slow motion. I was praying Tiffany didn't jump on the stage. I know I wouldn't be able to hold her back. Junior started recording Tony with his phone.

"Boy, what are you doin'?" Mama said.

"Aunt Hope, recording as proof Tony is alive. Just in case we need to show the popo if they come knockin' at Tiffany's door again accusing her of killin' Tony. Trust me, if the popo think you're involved in some mess, they won't stop until they arrest you." Junior said.

Everyone was watching Tony's reaction to Tiffany, but I was watching my sister's reaction. Tiffany walked past twice and stood front and center. Tony didn't notice her as far as I could tell.

Leah asked, "Tiff what do you plan to do? She doesn't recognize you. That's good. It means she doesn't remember, and the mind sweep is still workin'."

"Or it could mean that the bitch is fakin'. I need to know for sure. I'll wait for her to finish." Tiff said.

The fellas split into two groups and waited by both sides of the stage. We didn't know what side she would exit. Mama asked Tiffany what she wanted to do.

Tiffany said, "Mama you could touch her hands and see inside her mind. You'll be able to tell whether she remembers what happened or fakin'."

"I just can't walk up on her and grab her hands without scaring her." Mama said.

Junior said, "Aunt Hope you can act like a fan by shaking her hand and wanting to take a picture with her."

We all agreed. We all waited as Tony continue to sing two more songs. The waitin' was killin' us. I held Tiffany's hand because I didn't know what was going through her mind. Tony thanked everyone especially, Black for giving her this opportunity. She headed in the direction of Uncle Mac and Junior. We all cut through the crowd quickly. She was headed towards Black's tent.

"Drew" Mama yelled. Tony slowly turned around. "You have a beautiful voice my dear." Mama continued. Mama extended her hand as she walked closer to Tony. Tony politely smiled and said thank you. Mama asked if she could get a picture with her. Tony was very excited. Tony looks a lot different from our last encounter. She slimmed down. Her skin tone wasn't as bright and shiny or healthy. She no longer has locks but little twist that needed conditioner and oil. She had big bags under her eyes. I noticed a scar on her forearm that wasn't there before. She looked like she was barely makin' it. Mama shook her hand while Uncle Joe took the picture.

"Are you from here?" Mama asked.

Tony politely replied, "Yeah."

Tiffany demanded, "What part? You don't talk like you're from here. Whose yo family?"

"Do I know you?" Tony asked.

Tiffany was getting pissed. I stepped in front of Tiffany and said, "You just look like someone we know. No worries. We enjoyed your show."

"I see you guys met Drew," Black said.

Mama said, "Yes we were just telling your artists how much we enjoyed her show. But we were leaving because we have to fly out tomorrow."

"How do you guys know Black?" asked Tony

Uncle Mac said, "We all grew up together. So who're yo folks?"

Tony said, "My folks died when I was younger. I don't remember too much about them."

Mama said, "Well, we gotta go. Take care Tim." The fellas shook hands and said their goodbyes. We all headed back towards the vans. Our family stones began to light up.

"Tony was lyin'. When I touched her hand, I saw her thoughts. She knows we're looking for her. It's like she has been waiting. So the mind sweep didn't work." said Mama.

Tiffany said, "We should have killed her when we had the chance!"

"We're not killers." Mama said.

"So what the hell do we do now that we know she's fakin'?" said Uncle Joe.

"Not a Damn Thang!" Yelled Tony while pointing a gun at Leah's waist. Tony pulled Leah close and told all of us to walk towards the street away from the crowd.

Tiffany shouted, "There's the Bitch I know! If you think you get a second chance to try and kill us, you ARE crazy!"

"You don't want to do this. You will lose or worse." I told her.

"You've got some nerve after what you did to me, burning down my family's house and killing my parents!" Tony said.

Uncle Joe yelled, "Hold on gal! I don't know what the hell yo ass is talkin' bout! You got it wrong. It was yo dumb ass tryin' to kill us. Yo ass must be still high!" We were all tryin' to figure out what she was talkin' about. Tony had this puzzled look on her face as well. We didn't know what to think but she still had the gun on Leah.

Mama said these words quickly:

"By the ancestors that came before us
And the gifts that have been placed in our trust
I bind you with love and all the spirits might
I pray you listen with your ears and not by sight
May the wind slow down time this very night
And wisdom is shown in our site"

Our family stones began to shine brighter. The wind began to blow hard. Everyone around us was frozen in time including Tony. She could no longer hold the gun. Uncle Mac threw the gun in the trash after wiping his prints off. As Mama began to approach Tony, you could see the fear in her eyes.

Uncle Mac asked, "What was Tony talkin'? Some fire burning down her house and killing her parents? This bitch is crazy. We dropped her ass off on Decatur Street in the Quarters and got the hell up out of there."

As Mama held Tony's hand, she said, "She's living someone else's nightmare. These things didn't happen to her directly. She may have witnessed different things at different times, or someone related to her experience this. Either way, we know it wasn't us."

Tiffany walked up to her and straight hit her in the throat and said, "Yo ass won't be singin' no more songs or anything else for that matter."

I pulled Tiffany back as she's going to swing a second time. Tony was dumbfounded. She had no idea why Tiffany hit her.

Mama looked at Tony and said, "Tony you've been through a lot but what you've been through is not your story, maybe parts of it. But please believe me when I say we had nothing to do with the pain of your past. Most importantly we forgive you."

"Wait What! Hold the hell on! Like hell we do forgive this crazy girl! She tried to kill us! Hope, I know you saved and all, but the Lord is still workin' on some of us. We should have taken care of her ass for good the first time. Now we can finish the job." Uncle Joe said.

Mama said, "But she didn't kill us. We only came here for one purpose, to see if she was alive. Junior, did you get the pictures and video of Tony on stage with the date and time? That's all the proof we need that she's alive. The rest is in God's hands."

Junior said, "Yes Ma'am. I could take some more now if you need me to."

"No, we have enough. It's time to go." Mama said. As we walked away, Tony continued to sit on the ground clueless. As we pulled off in the van, Mama touched her stone, and it began to rain. Gram-T's favorite weather. Everyone returned to normal. During the ride home, Uncle Joe said we should have taken care of Tony because now she thinks we killed her parents in a burning house. Mama reassured all of us that once she touched Tony's hand and told her we forgave her, Tony knew the truth, that we had nothing to do with this tragedy and her heart changed towards us.

# Chapter Four

## Wasn't Me

We all headed back to Georgia the next morning. By the time we all got home, Junior had sent the video and pictures of Tony to us to have as proof just in case the police came to Tiffany's door again. The question still remains, who was Jane Doe in the shallow grave related to Tony? I ran some errands before heading to the salon. Later I picked up some Chinese food on the way home for dinner. I really missed Eric. Will probably eat while watching a couple of movies and then get X- rated.

The next morning I called Tiffany to check on her. She didn't say anything on the way back home from Louisiana. She said she was okay, but she still could kill Tony's ass. She said she was tired of everybody asking if she was okay. Even Junior offered to go find Tony and choke the hell out of her. I asked what she said because Junior is that crazy and will do it. He's like his daddy, Uncle Mac. He's the one to call to take care of the crazy shit.

Tiffany laughed and said, "I told him, I'm good and don't kill nobody."

It was good to hear her laugh. Deidra, my sorority line sistah, called me. She is another crazy one and will tell you in a minute. She's from Gary Indiana or G.I. as she calls it, and proud of it. Before I could get a word in, this is what Deidra shared, "Girrl, I'm getting married. This time, it's to a real man and not like that first bastard I married. He's from Chicago, Chi-town. He's an attorney which works in my favor because if I have to cut some damn body, he'll be able to defend me. Ree, when I tell you he got that good lovin'… Shit, he turned me out! He has one son, that's seven years old. He's cool. Even the little boy's mama, his ex-wife is cool. I met her once. He keeps the drama out completely."

I asked, "So have you set a date, and does he want more kids?"

"Sands were going to the Bahamas for a small private ceremony with just a few other couples who can afford to go, his mom and maybe my parents. I hope you and Eric can come. We're going in August which is in a few months." she said.

I said, "Dee, I'm so excited for you. You didn't answer the question about him wanting kids. Does he want kids?"

Deidra screamed, "Sands, I'm pregnant. Why do you think we're going to the Bahamas as soon as we can? So I can be the baddest bitch on the beach before my belly pops out and my breasts grow to the size of cantaloupes. I'm about two months but we're not telling people yet. But you know I had to tell my girl. You gotta meet Keith soon. He has some business in Atlanta next month. We'll all plan to get together then. Ree, I'm so happy." We talked for about another hour.

The next week was busy at both salons. It was getting hot once again here in Georgia. I hired two braiders for each salon. Georgia has the worst humidity, so now sistahs want a convenient hairstyle that can withstand the heat. It's too hot for wigs and weaves. I keep my hair braided during the summer months. Eric loves my individual braids down my back especially when I'm butt naked. Kim and I braided hair more than wash and sets. Nothing's worse than paying to have your hair done and sweating the curls out an hour later. Braiding hair came naturally to me since I was a kid. I got a hook up in purchasing virgin human hair and synthetic hair to make my own personalized ponytails and wigs for clients. The ponytails and wigs are becoming a huge business as well by themselves. That was a smart investment. With the money I'm making from ponytails and wigs, I paid off our car debts along with other debts. We were able to pay for a nice vacation for Mama and Daddy. We are truly blessed. The third Saturday in each month, we donate money to the church to help feed the homeless. Daddy even fires up the grill and we pass out food in the church parking lot. I have so much to be thankful for. Eric was in the ICU after the terrible stabbin' on our wedding day, the doctors didn't know if he was going to make it. A couple of times they had to resuscitate him as I watched in horror. They had to take me out of the room. For a while, I was angry with God. He let this happen to Eric. He didn't deserve it. He was a good man. Maybe I was being punished for sleeping with Jonathan before we were married. I was angry with myself because I did the unforgivable thing. Shit, it wasn't even worth it. I asked God to forgive me for betraying Eric, lying to myself, my family, and the police. I cried for days straight not knowing what

*Blood, Secrets and Lies 2 The Grave*

was gonna happen to Eric. I pondered if I should tell him or not. I decided not to tell a soul. I didn't want to risk losing Eric. Men aren't as forgiving as women. Even though it was before we married, it would crush him. Eric and I talked about forgiveness, but we didn't talk about the betrayal and lies. Tiffany said, "Take that shit to the grave!" He had to have therapy for several months. He was in so much pain, all I could think about, was how I was responsible. Inside I knew something was wrong the day of the wedding. I thought it was the typical wedding day chaos. I was wrong.

I went to the salon the next morning early. Tiffany came in right behind me. She looked well rested finally. I washed and trimmed her locks. I told her about Deidra's good news. We both laughed about how crazy Deidra can be. Just as we were reminiscing about college, a woman walked in, that I didn't recognize. I asked if she was here for Kim, but she said no. She said she was here to see me. She looked upset. I asked if she had an appointment. She said nothin'.

Tiffany turned around and said, "Ah my sister asked do you have an appointment or is there somethin' else you want?"

"So you're the woman he can't seem to get over!" the woman replied.

I demanded, "What the hell did you say?!"

She said, "He never mentioned me?"

Tiff yelled, "Ah no bitch, nobody mentioned you! What the hell are you talkin' about?!

"Really Renee, Jonathan never mentioned me? I'm Tasha!" The woman yelled.

"Okay, what the hell do you want?! I asked.

She said, "I love Jonathan, but no he still loves yo ass. And he's in jail cause of you. And he won't be getting out anytime soon."

Tiff cut her off, "No bitch, you got that all wrong. He's in jail because of the crazy shit HE did. Who goes around stabbin' people?! And if you knew he still loves Ree, why in the hell were you with him like a fool?"

She turned towards Tiffany and said, "You need to stay the hell out of this. This ain't got nothin' to do with you."

I stepped closer to her and calmly said, "You might wanna back up and get the hell out of here.

I have nothin' to do with that bastard. Trust me when I say, don't come back. It won't end well for you."

The fire in my eyes must have scared her because she left quickly.

Tiff asked, "Did you know that crazy chick?"

I said, "Naw I don't know her or any of the other women Jonathan had strung by the nose. That's why I left his ass along we were in school. There was always drama around him. I don't think she'll be back."

Tiff asked, "Did she see your eyes?"

We both laughed. Because of our bloodline, when we are threatened, or our mood changes, our family stone changes colors along with our eyes. You really don't notice unless you are up close to us, or you really piss us off.

The rest of the day went by quickly. Eric called and said he was picking up Mexican food around the corner for dinner. When I got home the table was set. I was starvin'. I didn't tell Eric about the crazy girl who came into the salon. I don't want to bring up anything that has to do with Jonathan. Of course he asked how the day went. I just told him it was busy. Eric was on his way to the shower and asked if I would join him. I was so damn tired. I told him, I'll make it up to him tomorrow. I just put my PJs on and crashed.

I got a call from Mama early the next morning sayin' to meet her, Daddy, Tiff, and the attorney at the police station. The detective wanted to ask more questions. We all arrived at the same time. We made sure we had the pictures and video with the date of Tony in New Orleans.

The attorney said, "Tony's sister is claiming she has a recording of Tiffany threatening Tony."

We all knew that was a lie because everything was all good up until the family get together when Tony tried to kill us. We all sat in the detective's office.

Out of nowhere, we hear Tony's crazy sister yellin' through the glass window, "I know you killed my Tony! You took her away from me! She loved me!"

She was escorted to another room. The detective said there was a message left on the answering machine of a woman threatening Tony over some money. They need Tiffany to read a script to see if her voice matches.

The attorney interrupted, "You mean rule out Tiffany. We need to hear the message first to see if the voices are similar. And for the record, my client has a good career and makes nice money. So she doesn't need to threaten anyone over money. We keep talking about Ms. Tony, but what about the Jane Doe that is actually dead that has the family DNA, or did you forget about her?"

Mama said, "I've had enough of this crazy talk from Tony's sister, saying Tiffany killed Tony. This poor Jane Doe is in the morgue, and no one knows what happened to her. Tony is alive and I have proof!"

The detective and the attorney were shocked.

Mama said, "We were in Louisiana visiting family and went to an outdoor concert. Guess who was the headliner? Alive and in the flesh, Tony." Mama pulled her phone out along with a USB flash memory stick with the video and photos and showed the attorney as he passed the phone to detectives. The date and time were clear.

The attorney said, "Well as you can see, Tony isn't dead. All investigations towards my client are done. Please inform her sister, so she can move on and try to find out which relative is in the morgue.

My client is free of any charges or allegations and is not to be harassed by you, this department or Tony's sister, Sherry, again."

I asked, "So who is the crazy girl on the answering machine sounding nothin' like Tiffany?"

The detective said they were still looking into it and that we were all free to go.

As we were leaving, Tony's sister, Sherry came towards us yelling, "Where is Tony?!"

Tiffany whipped out her phone showing the video of Tony on stage singing. Sherry began to dance off beat I might add. She even started laughin'. Somethin' is seriously wrong with this lady. Somethin' in her eyes was telling me there was more to her.

Then she had the nerve to say, "Oops."

"Hell naw! Bitch you accuse me of murder, and I showed you proof that Tony ain't dead, and all you got to say is, Oops!" Tiffany yelled.

Mama grabbed Tiffany's hand and said we needed to go. None of us cursed in front of our parents even though we were adults. But this bitch was pushin' it. Tiff turned toward Mama and Daddy and apologize for cursing.

Mama extended her hand to Sherry and said, "I'm glad Tony is okay and I'm so sorry for the loss of your family member."

Sherry tried to hug Mama, but I stepped in front to intervene. I didn't trust her. Mama just reached for her hand. Sherry shook Mama's hand and smiled the most devilish smile. Mama's expression on her face changed and so did the color of our family stones. Somethin' is terribly wrong.

Mama said while still holding Sherry's hand, "It was you. You killed that girl, your own family!

**"Red is the color of blood that was shed**

**Open our eyes and minds of what was said**

**Reveal the truth that holds the key**

**Stop this moment in time so we may be free."**

All of our stones change from purple to red. It became dark in the police station. Not even the emergency lights were on. Everyone else was frozen in time including Daddy for his own protection. The only light that was shinin' came from our stones. The rain came down hard while lightning lit up the sky. You could hear the thunder like a loud roar. Sherry stood there clueless with a dumb look on her face. Mama had the gift of touch. She can see a person's past, present and future with just a touch. Some may consider this a curse. But Mama used it only when necessary.

Tiffany yelled, "Yo whole family is…."

"Don't Tiff," Mama said as she turned back towards Sherry. "Why would you do such a terrible thing to your own family? What in the world did she do to deserve being pushed down a whole flight of stairs and thrown in a grave?"

Sherry had a smirk on her face with no remorse in her eyes and calmly said, "Well, since you asked. They all deserved to die. They didn't love me, they loved her more. I loved her too. She really loved me and only me. They knew it. They hated that she loved me. When they took me away from her, it shattered my world. The rooms were so small I couldn't breathe. They were always shoving pills down my throat. I would sleep for days and days. I would wake up in my own piss. When I asked where she was, they just ignored me. Do you know what it feels like to be ignored? She loved only me, and they took her away from me. But that's okay."

Finally, I demanded, "Who are you talkin' about the girl in the morgue?" As I pulled my cell phone to record to give to the police.

She had an evil look on her face. She smiled and said, "Oh her, naw. That bitch needed to die. She's the reason I was in and out of those white padded rooms. She needed to die. She took away my baby sister who was the one who loved me. Laura loved me when we were kids. I would twist her hair, read stories to her, and draw pictures for her. Until that awful day. All of us kids were playin' outside. We took turns swingin' each other around. Tony was swingin' Laura so hard, that she swung Laura up against a tree. She didn't move. We all started screamin'. Daddy came runnin' outside yellin', "What happened?!" No one said a word. He looked at me and said, "You did this, didn't you?!" Before I could answer, Tony's mom came runnin' out screamin' and yellin', "Get the hell away from my baby!" Shortly after the ambulance and the police came, I was taken to a special hospital with padded rooms before I could tell them it wasn't me. My mama was sick and couldn't take care of me. But as time went on, no one came for me. I played nice for many years and got out. I heard Tony and her family were movin'. I had to pay them a visit during the night. Tony was at one of the neighbors for sleepover which I didn't know. I set their house on fire. Tony's mama, her brother, and my daddy all died. They didn't love me. So they needed to die. The house went up in flames so quickly. I could hear them screamin', but I was screamin' when they dragged me off. Nobody helped me. You shouldn't ignore people. Oh well."

Tiffany said, "What the hell! You know Tony is alive?! So who in the hell did you kill that's in the morgue and why?!"

"Oh that sorry bitch! That was my cousin, Wanda. She was always jealous of me and Laura. Wanda was the person who also saw Tony swing Laura into the tree and didn't say a word. She pointed to me when daddy asked what happened. She blamed me for my sweet baby sister's death. She's the reason, I was taken away. By killin' her, I hoped it would bring Tony home, after all Tony did kill Laura and she needs to pay for what she did too. So many guilty people, don't you think?"

Tiffany yelled, "Damn, all y'all need to be put down SHIT!"

Sherry said, "Well I guess the cat is out of the bag. We can tell the detectives to go get my sister Tony because she needs to pay for her sins. She needs to repent. I killed my triflin' cousin to help my half-sister Tony, atone for what she did, then I can forgive her. Then we can be a family again."

Tiffany said, "Who are you to say Tony needs to repent after all the crazy stuff you did?!"

The Bible says, "Repent, then turned to God." Sherry said.

"The Bible also says, whoever conceals their sins does not prosper, but the one who confesses and renounces them finds mercy. You got caught so there would be no mercy for you if I had my way you dumbass." Tiffany said.

That's one thing about us, we all were raised in the church, and we know our Bible, especially Tiffany. She may try and kill you slowly, but then she'll pray for your soul and ask for forgiveness of her sins as well.

"Are you always this angry? Maybe you should take anger management classes, my dear." Sherry said.

"Bitch, keep talkin'! Tiffany shouted back.

Just then the spell was broken, and the lights came on. The rain suddenly stopped. Everyone heard Sherry say she killed her cousin, and she knew Tony was alive. She even said it again. This crazy chick thinks what she did, was okay. They handcuffed her and took her away. This crazy girl had the nerve to say, "Would y'all call Tony and tell her to come get me?"

Tiffany just rolled her eyes at her. Mama felt sorry for her. Mom also explained, this is what Tony was talking about in Louisiana. When Tony's mind was swept clean, she remembered pieces from the past. That's the crazy thing about the mind sweeps, you don't know how the person will be affected and that's what makes it dangerous. We all left.

# *Chapter Five*

## No Party For Me

*L*eah called with Tiffany on the line to ask if we would be interested in joining the local women's softball league. Not only do the women in our family have special gifts in our blood line, but we come from a long line of athletes. Mama and Auntie played basketball. Faith, Mama's oldest sister who died tragically when she was young, ran track and swam. Even Uncle Mac and Uncle Joe played football. Tiffany, Leah, and I played softball and volleyball. But the most famous athlete in our family was Gram-T. She played softball. We always spent our summers in Louisiana with Gram-T and Grandpa Jerry. This particular summer, I remember being tired of playin' hopscotch, double dutch and hide and go seek. Gram-T told us to go into the shed to find an old box. Inside the box, we found baseball gloves, a faded baseball cap, an old volleyball net, three big baseballs, several trophies and newspaper clippings. We were so excited we thought we found gold. She told us to bring it to her, the three balls with the two gloves. Each dirty old ball had the number, "13" on it. I could tell there was somethin' special about the baseball gloves and cap.

Like every curious child, I asked, "Whose is these, Mama and Auntie?"

Gram-T laughed and told us to go get some sweet tea and come sit on the back porch so she could tell us who they belong to.

This was her story, "The big puffy glove as you called it, is the catcher's mitt and it belongs to me. The other glove belongs to your Grandpa Jerry. And these big baseballs are called softballs. I was a member of the first softball league for colored women."

Leah being about seven years old and naïve asked, "What color team was you on? I like yellow. These balls don't feel so soft. They are really hard, Gram-T."

Gram-T smiled and said, "No baby, colored women referred to the color of our skin. Sometimes we were called Negroes as well. Leah's smile

*Blood, Secrets and Lies 2 The Grave*

quickly turned into a frown. We were all taught at an early age about racism and segregation growin' up in the south.

Gram-T continued, "I was about fourteen or fifteen when the league had tryouts. I wasn't the tallest, but I was fast and could catch any ball thrown my way. So they made me a catcher. The number on my jersey was 13. We played against some of the best female players in the league. We even practice with men baseball players. They weren't too happy playin' with us gals because we were just as good. They thought the women should be in the kitchen not in the field playin' ball. There were more white teams than black. Segregation made it hard to play at times. We had to be careful of some of the towns we played in, especially at night. During that time, Blacks weren't welcome everywhere. But for some strange reason, the white folks love to come out and see us play. Can you imagine, white folks comin' to see colored girls play ball? People wanted us to play in a skirt. But one of my teammates said, "We're playin' ball not baking cookies. And if people are going to take us seriously, we need to look like real ballplayers." We always had a full house every game.

Leah asked, "Did you win the championship Gram-T?"

Gram-T smiled and said, "I'm getting to that part baby. We won all of our games so far. We had a chance to play this team in Gary Indiana. Our local church made overnight arrangements for us to stay with other black families in Indiana. Back then, there were no hotels that allowed Blacks to sleep in them, but we were only allowed to work in them. I'll never forget the team's name, "The Steel City Chicks." They won all of their games up to this point like us. The stadium was packed with Blacks and whites. I couldn't believe my eyes this stadium was nice. They even allow us to use the locker rooms. Most of the time we had to change clothes on the bus because we weren't allowed to use the facilities. God was smiling down on all of us. Both teams were coming out of the locker room at the same time. We all smiled because we all knew this was a special moment in time. I heard one of the other girls on the other team ask their catcher, "How you feelin' Jack?" I thought that was strange. We use the name Jack in reference to a man. But she responded, "I feel great." They both started walking off as I saw the catcher's last name on the back of her shirt. Her last name was, Jack. We both had the same number 13 on our jerseys.

*Blood, Secrets and Lies 2 The Grave*

I ran up to her and introduce myself. She was very friendly and said, "I'm Anna Jack. Good luck to you ladies." I said thanks, same to you. It seemed like that was the hardest and longest game of my life. These girls were good. To hear the white folks cheer so hard was amazing. That was a once in a lifetime moment back then."

Tiffany shouted with her little self, "Did you win the prize Gram-T?"

Gram-T smiled, "No baby the other team won. But it was one of the best times of my life. And I made a few friends along the way. Anna Jack and I kept in touch. She became a wife, mama, and a nurse. I even taught yo Grandpa Jerry how to catch a curve ball."

Leah asked, "Gram-T were you famous? Did they put your picture on a cereal box?"

Gram-T said, "I was famous here in New Orleans. But there was one famous black female baseball player. Her name was Toni Stone. She was one of three women to play professional baseball in the Negro league. She played baseball while I played softball, so we never played against each other. But I heard she was somethin' to see. She even got a hit off Satchel Paige. He was a famous black male pitcher in my time."

I loved sitting outside on the porch drinkin' lemonade or sweet tea with my sisters listenin' to Gram-T share her life's journey. People don't understand how important our elders are until they are gone. But we cherished those times. I loved soakin' up the wisdom from my elders, not just Gram-T and Grandpa Jerry, but my Sunday school teacher, my coach and my elementary teacher, Ms. Reed just to name a few.

Tiffany said she needed to release some tension since beating a murder rap. So she planned on joining the softball team. I still haven't decided yet. I was still working long hours at the salon and Eric was at the gym most of the week. Playin' softball again would give me some form of exercise. I told Leah I'll let her know by the end of the week.

I spoke to Sandra the next day. She asked if we all were coming down for Uncle Mac's birthday party next month. Although he said he didn't want a birthday party, we're just calling it the usual, "family get together." I told her Eric and I will probably come. I said I would ask everyone else and let her know. I know how it is to plan a party. You need a headcount, how much food to order and bottles of liquor to bring. Mama and Daddy are always up for going back home to see family. They may even drive. They love road trips. You would think after all those hot road trips in the family van, they will be tired of driving. I even offered to pay for their airline tickets, but they always turned us down. It's because of those road trips, I get on the first plane out. I called both Leah and Tiffany to see if they were going to Louisiana. Leah said she might, and Tiffany said she didn't know yet. I know Tiffany needed a break from all of the chaos but that's the family life we live.

We all decided to join Mama and Daddy this Sunday for family day at church. After church, we'll have dinner following. She said she and Daddy would take care of everything. When Eric came home, I asked him if he would like to join my family for church and Sunday dinner as I stood there butt ass naked in these red high-heeled shoes. I knew I would get a yes for sure.

He smiled and said, "Baby I'm sorry what did you ask me? Did you ask me about church? We both laughed.

I asked again and he responded, "Hell yeah."

I got to the salon early. Kim was right behind me. She starts her day, just as early as I do. Kim is a hard worker. I am so blessed to work with her. She's come a long way. I remember when I first met her. I thought to myself, I don't have time to babysit. But I was very wrong. Kim turned out to be the best stylist in both salons. Always in early and the last to leave. She can do hair like nobody's business. She's married to a good man now. Unlike the little troll she was living with when I first met her. I'm so proud of her. She said her goal was to get her own salon by next year. Knowing her, she'll get it before then. We finished the last of our clients. I invited her and her family to come to Mama's church on Sunday. She said she was going to her grandmother's church.

Sunday came fast. The entire family was waiting in the family life Center. The junior ushers were tryin' to find seats for all of us. It was funny to see the look in their eyes tryin' to find six seats together. Finally, the little boy said, "Y'all need to find yo own seats. They didn't show me how to do this many people. It's time for my snack, bye."

We laughed and found our own seats. The children's choir lined up at the altar. I tried not to laugh but Tiffany kept making faces. Even Leah

*Blood, Secrets and Lies 2 The Grave*

held her head down to keep from laughin'. The kids' choir was funny. Half of the kids were rockin' in the wrong direction. Some kids were clappin' while others just stood there. One kid said he needed to go sit on the pot.

Mama pointed to me saying, "Ree that was you and Leah always having to go to the bathroom at the wrong time." The sermon was short and sweet from a visiting pastor.

As soon as we all got to the house, we were all starvin'. We placed the food in the oven while we change clothes. Daddy smoked a turkey and a ham the night before. Mama made some dressin', greens, fried corn, mac and cheese, potato salad and lemon pound cake. We ate like no tomorrow. We discussed who was going to Uncle Mac's birthday celebration in Louisiana. It looks like it was just Mama, Daddy, Eric, and I were going. Leah had a lot of work to do and wasn't going. Tiffany just didn't feel like being bothered. By the time Eric and I got home we were tired and laid around the rest of the evening. I went on and booked our airline tickets for Louisiana. Sandra already said Eric and I could stay with her, and they would pick us up from the airport.

I had two weddings and a woman's retreat for church in the coming weeks. I moved my schedule around for my weekly clientele for my Uncle's party. Meanwhile, I was tryin' to figure out what to get Uncle Mac for his birthday. I know he doesn't want anything, but we never go to anyone's house empty-handed. I'll probably get him a gift card, somethin' I can throw in my suitcase. Speaking of a suitcase, it was time to pack. I always over packed for my trips. I'll pull out my biggest luggage while Eric uses a simple duffel bag. I called Mama and told her I'll get Uncle Mac a gift card from all of us. She reminded me once again, that he doesn't like gifts.

"Why doesn't Uncle Mac like parties or gifts? Who doesn't want to be celebrated? You know I love a good party and a good cake." I asked. Mama became quiet.

Mama said, "Ree, Mac really doesn't like sharing his reasons for not liking parties. But I'll share with you so you can calm down. When we were teenagers, mama decided to throw Mac a birthday party for his eighteenth birthday. The entire family was invited, along with some of the neighborhood and Mac's classmates. Also, this girl named Sarah. They just started datin'. She was gorgeous, smart, quiet and Mac was crazy about her. We all liked her and so did all the other guys. She moved to NOLA from Mississippi. But there was somethin' about her that I just couldn't put my finger on. Not that she was bad, but she was hiding somethin'. Mac would always tell me to leave it alone. So I did. The other kids at the party started drinking including Joe and Mac. Some guy out of nowhere stumbles on Mac and says, "Congratulations boy you got the prize, two for one. Everybody has been tryin' to get in Sarah's pants. But you are the only one. A toast to big Dick Mac." Joe pushed him away and told him to leave. The expression on Mac's face, said he didn't know what the guy was talkin' about. The drunk boy just laughed and pointed to Sarah's belly. Mac punches the boy in the face and a fight broke out. Papa pulled out his shotgun and told everyone to leave. Mac looks at Sarah and demanded to know what was going on. Mac hadn't slept with Sarah at all. Sarah had tears in her eyes. She didn't say a word. Mac was pissed. He told her to leave. She left her sweater behind. I told Mac to take it to her, but he threw it on the ground and went into the house. Mama picked up the sweater that night to do a revealing spell. I didn't know at the time. She found out Sarah's awful truth. Sarah's father was killed in a bar fight when she was a little girl. Her mama married the bastard who killed her father not knowing. The rumors and talk about him killing her father being a setup kept surfacing. So he moved Sarah and her mom here to Louisiana. But the truth followed. Sarah's stepfather killed her father not to have her mom, but Sarah. Sarah was pregnant by her stepfather. The sick bastard was raping Sarah. She didn't tell a soul not even her mama. Mac was furious when Mama told him. It took Papa and Mama to calm him down. The next morning Papa and Mac went to Sarah's house to confront her stepfather. When they got there, police cars were there. The police weren't allowing anyone to enter the house. Mac pushed his way through the crowd with Papa right behind him demanding to see Sarah. The police told him no one was allowed in. Sarah's mom was in a police car sobbing like a baby. Sarah's stepfather was handcuffed in another police car. Mac yelled for Sarah to come out. But she didn't. Finally, the police came over and asked who Mac was. Papa explained that Mac was a good friend of Sarah's. The police escorted Papa and Mac to the other side of the crowd asking a lot of questions. Mac yelled, "Where is Sarah?! I need to see her!" As Mac pushed past the police, two people came out of the house carrying a body bag. Another police officer grabbed Mac from behind, as Mac tries to see if it was Sarah.

Papa grabbed Mac away from the police officer and asked, "Please officer this is my son. He is a friend of Sarah's. Is that Sarah being carried out?"

The officer shook his head and said, "Yes, I'm sorry."

Mac and Papa couldn't believe it. Sarah's mom found her in the bed holding a picture of Mac and Sarah that they recently took right after shooting herself. She left a note for her mom telling her everything about her evil stepfather. It took Mac a while to get over everything. He blamed himself for her death. Mac went to Alabama to stay with Uncle John for a while."

Damn!!! I didn't know what to say after that.

July is hot as hell in Louisiana. Sandra was there to pick us up from the airport. She looked fabulous. Her hubby Phil was at home with the twins. I couldn't wait to see all of the family, eat the best food in town, and hear the craziest stories. As we pulled up to the house, two little kids were wavin' in the window. As soon as we walked in, the two little ones ran to their mommy and became shy when I tried to hug them. They eventually warmed up. Phil had the spread laid out. We ate well. Mama called to see if we had arrived. I decided to give the gift card that was originally for Uncle Mac to Auntie to help with the cost of the food.

While Sandra and I were cleaning the kitchen, Phil and Eric were in the family room drinkin' and watchin' a game on TV. Suddenly I felt a poke at my leg. I turned to look down and saw the twins run off gigglin'. We all laugh. I asked if we needed to help with the cookin' for tomorrow. Sandra said the elders would take care of it. Usually, when we have a get together, we all pitch in. But if they got it, I'm good.

# Chapter Six

## Those Eyes

Today the family is hangin' at Auntie's house and on Saturday we're all going to Uncle Joe's house. We had more additions to the family. Even old friends from the neighborhood were here. The yard was packed. The food was done by the time everyone arrived. There were lots of faces I didn't recognize. Auntie said she invited Mrs. Bebe's family to join. Mrs. Bebe was one of Gram-T's good friends who live down the street. Mrs. Bebe's daughter, June and what looked like her entire family was here. Ms. June was older than Mama and 'em but her beautiful brown tight skin, auburn colored hair and bright white teeth made her look younger.

Uncle Joe laughed and said, "She's a nice old lady but can turn a bottle up in a minute and won't stop talkin'."

It was too late. I turned around she had a cup in her hand with brown liquor filled to the top. Daddy and I were standing there laughin' at her.

She motioned for me to come over and said, "You Mrs. Thelma's granddaughter? Hey Daniel, you still lookin' good."

Daddy just smiled. I politely smiled and told her yes that Gram-T was my grandmother. Uncle Mac came over with a plate of food to offer to Ms. June. She was too busy enjoyin' her drink. She talked loud, laughed loud, and sang loud.

She turned the food down and said, "I got all I need in this cup for now. I see you still got those strange eyes, you and yo brotha Joe."

Then she had the nerve to start gyrating next to Uncle Mac. Uncle Mac just smiled and left the plate while walking away irritated. She introduced me to the rest of her family, a very outspoken bunch of people. They talked loud as well. Sandra finally came over to rescue me.

*Blood, Secrets and Lies 2 The Grave*

Sandra said, "Don't pay her no mind. As you can see, she loves her liquor and loves to gossip." Sandra said she and Phil were planning to come to Georgia right after the holidays. Just as we were making plans, we heard Mama fussin' with Uncle Mac. Apparently, Ms. June had said somethin' to Uncle Mac that pissed him off. I walked over to see what was goin' on.

Uncle Mac yelled at Ms. June, "Look. You need to stop drinkin' because now you're talkin' crazy, and you don't know what the hell you're talkin' about!"

Uncle Joe came over to try and calm Uncle Mac down, but it was too late.

"You know I know the truth. Yeah, you and yo brotha know I know. Look at y'all and those eyes. Y'all got them eyes." Ms. June's daughters came over, took her cup from her, and said they were leaving. But Ms. June refused to leave. I recalled the last get together when all of the shit hit the fan, I noticed Uncle Mac's eyes. His eyes had a strange appearance of fire and when I questioned him, he just laughed. What was Ms. June tryin' to say? What did their eyes have to do with anything? Her son was cross eyed. When you were talkin' to him, you didn't know if he was looking at you or the person next to you. In our family, we all have different color eyes. Maybe they have glaucoma. So what!

"You two really don't know? "Ms. June said as she pointed to Uncle Mac and Uncle Joe.

Uncle Joe yelled back, "What the hell are you gossipin' about now? Shit git somewhere and sit yo ass down! Naw better yet, you need to git yo drunk ass out now!"

Ms. June fired back, "I may be drunk, but I know some shit. Yo precious mama, Thelma Sullivan, wasn't always a saint. The proof is in those eyes."

Auntie said, "Take her home, she's had too much to drink."

"Yeah, I'm drunk and none of y'all know the truth." Ms. June laughed.

Uncle Joe said, "What you say bout my mama?!"

Talkin' about somebody's mama can get you killed especially when you're talkin' to Uncle Mac and Uncle Joe. They worship the ground Gram-T walked on.

Ms. June said, "I guess it's true what they say, take it to the grave."

Her family dragged her out as her grandson sincerely apologized. I could tell by the look on his face their entire family was embarrassed. Everyone just brushed her off as the neighborhood drunk. Mama, Auntie, Uncle Mac, and Uncle Joe were in a huddle yellin' back and forth at each other. Why was this woman talkin' badly about Gram-T? Now she was talkin' about my Uncles as well. Damn, what the hell are they hiding this time?! These damn secrets are gonna kill us all. But I need to know... Or do I?

After the shit show from Ms. June, everyone eventually left. Mama, Uncle Joe, and Uncle Mac went into the house. The rest of us help clean up and put away the food. I think we were all walkin' on eggshells, tryin' not to listen, but I wanted to know what the hell was goin' on. Finally, Uncle Joe came outside smokin' a cigar. We know he's gonna say somethin' crazy. But he didn't say a word. I got nervous. I never wiped down a table so hard in my life tryin' to be invisible.

Uncle Mac came out of the house yellin', "I thought all that shit was in the past and forgotten. Her raggedy ass keeps bringin' shit up!"

"All man, June is still pissed you married Bernice over her drunk ass. You screwed that piece of trash once and she done lost her mind over you. Trash is always trash. The older it git, the more it stank." Joe said.

I was still wiping off the same damn table. I wanted to know more. Phil came out and said he was taking the kids home. I told Eric to go with them while Sandra and I finish cleaning. So they left.

"We should have cloaked her memory while we had the chance. Some people don't know how to keep their mouths shut." Uncle Mac said,

Oh shit, did he say, "Cloaked her memory?" What the hell!

Uncle Mac turned slowly at me and said, "Ree, I forgot you were standin' here. You good?"

I shook my head saying yes. I knew it. Some shit went down AGAIN. But this time, it's not me. Mama and Auntie came outside to check on the fellas. They all just sat for a moment sayin' nothin'.

Uncle Joe looked over at me asking, "Ree how long are you gonna keep wipin' that same damn table? Come sit down girl."

"I thought we left all that in the past, shit! Uncle Mac said.

"Mac it was in the past. It's just June being June." Auntie said

I politely cleared my throat trying to get their attention in hopes of clearing up this shit.

"Could someone please explain what's goin' on? You know, Ms. June and cloaking the memory." I said.

By this time, the sun went down. Uncle Joe lit the fire pit as we all gathered around.

Uncle Mac finally explains, "Y'all know when we were young, Ms. Bebe, mama's good friend had a couple of businesses including a boarding house. She even had a few famous people stayin' there especially jazz folks. That was the spot to be in. It was like a juke joint every night, good food, music, and moonshine. Me and Joe were regulars on Friday night. One night we ran into June. We all hung out together like we were runnin' the joint. But of course, June started thinkin' she was my woman. When I told her I didn't like her like that, she started hangin' with this jazz musician named Eddie. He was cool with all of the brothas, and the ladies loved him. He was just a little too slick for me, but June left me alone. One night, me and Joe were playin' dominoes with some of the fellas in the band and June ran past us pissed as hell. We didn't pay her no mine until Eddie came runnin' behind her lookin' crazy.

Joe interrupted, "That fool came runnin' behind her with his clothes halfway hangin' off beggin' her not to say nothin' bout what she saw."

Uncle Mac continued, "June slapped the shit out of Eddie and left out. We figured she caught him with another girl, and we kept on playin' dominoes. A couple of days later she had a black eye but wouldn't say how she got it. At this point, she stopped speaking to me and Joe. I guess she was still mad because I didn't want her. Joe said it probably was Eddie who hit her. June's older brother left for the Army. I know he would have slit Eddie's throat. But he wasn't here. So Joe made me feel bad and said we needed to check on her. We headed to the boarding house that night but on the way down the street, we heard screaming in the woods. It was June. Eddie had her on the ground beatin' her like a man. I grabbed him by the throat with one hand. Joe got June off the ground. But as Joe

*Blood, Secrets and Lies 2 The Grave*

was helping her up, she starts laughin' like a crazy person.

June said, "That mothafucka is the real bitch right there. He doesn't want y'all to know he's a bitch. Tell 'em, Eddie. Tell 'em, Eddie. You like balls in yo damn ass. I walked in on you and Sam goin' hard. You nasty mothafucka!"

As I was holding him up in the air, he kicked June in her face. That's when I lost it. Without knowing, I revealed myself to him at that moment."

I asked, "What do you mean you reveal yourself?"

Uncle Mac said, "Ree the blood runs through the men in the family too, not just the ladies."

As he turned around, his fired feel eyes appeared bright once again. As I remembered seeing them at the last get together, but I thought I was imagining things. They were brighter than the flames from the fire pit. There was also a glow around him as well. A tattoo in the corner of the web of his hand also glowed. I looked at Mama and demanded, "Why didn't you tell us? I thought it was just the women. But it's the men too. How come no one told us?!"

"It wasn't our place to tell their story." Mama said calmly. Auntie shook her head in agreement.

Sandra asked, "So do you have gifts? Do you get them at a certain age? Can you control the elements of the earth? Are you witches, warlocks or what are you called?"

"Y'all watch too much TV. We like to be called, Uncle Joe and Uncle Mac. But to the elders, we are called the guardians. But we don't need titles like you ladies."

Uncle Mac continued, "The gifts as you call them, come at the age of eighteen. We all have the family mark."

"What family mark are you talkin' about?" I asked.

He asked me to spread my hand flat. There was a strange mark in the web of the thumb that I never paid attention to. Then he overlapped his hand on top of my hand. I couldn't believe what I saw next. It was a small symbol like two swords crossing. I couldn't believe it. Whether it was Uncle Joe's or Uncle Mac's hand, the symbol formed no matter whose hand laid on top of ours. I even had Mama hold her hand with Uncle Mac and the symbol appeared. Wow.

*Blood, Secrets and Lies 2 The Grave*

Sandra asked, "So do you guys use spells, chants or have visions?"

"Naw, for us, it's a little different. Men and women are wired differently. Our ancestors give the men in our family strength through our minds, which in return gives us unique physical powers as well. We can control the elements as well. Yeah, we studied our family history, so to answer your questions yes, we are familiar with the chants and spells. We even know when you all use 'em." Uncle Joe said.

"So do you all have secret ceremonies with just the men?" I asked.

Uncle Joe answered, "You mean like your rose ceremony and wearing white that you ladies do?"

Sandra and I both looked at each other in shock. They knew.

"Who do you think slows down the time and stands guard to make sure no one interrupts your ceremony during the late-night hours?" Uncle Joe asked.

That's why I love our family. We always have each other's back even when we don't know. So Uncle Mac went back to telling us the story about June.

"Like I said I was holding up Eddie with one hand crushing his throat. Joe was helping June up when she saw our eyes and the marks on our hands bright as a light. June start yellin', "What the hell?! How the hell you holdin' that bastard up with one hand. Y'all eyes are glowin' in shit both of y'all. What's wrong with y'all? Take your hands off of me, Joe. I'm gettin' the hell out of here." So she ran so fast and hit a damn tree. She was out cold. Blood was all over her face. So now we had Eddie and June to deal with. We left Eddie and carried June back to the house and took her in the shed. We told mama everything. First, she stitched June's forehead. She put together a paste for June's bruises. Eddie messed her up badly. Mama also did a spell to erase June's memory for the night. We go back to the field where Eddie was, he was still knocked out. June was waking up when she saw mama doin' a mind sweep on Eddie. But we paid her know mind. Eddie woke up and couldn't speak. He was scared to death and didn't know what happened to him. He just ran off. June was in a daze. We walked her back. She couldn't remember anythin', so we thought. That was over thirty

*Blood, Secrets and Lies 2 The Grave*

years ago. But it seems like the spell has worn off. It doesn't matter, when you're known as the town drunk, ain't nobody gonna believe you."

Once again, I was speechless. I don't know whether to be in awe or pissed because somethin' else I didn't know bout the family. We all sat quietly for a moment. My head began to pound. I was tired and stuffed. We all decide to call it a night. Next thing I know, I heard someone yellin', "That's them, the Sullivans. Them voodoo mothafuckas. They all witches. Y'all put some kinda hex me. But I know what y'all did." June yelled.

We all turned around to find Ms. June standing there with a group of drunk roughnecks. I know this old bitch didn't think she was comin' to give my Uncles a beat down. All Hell Naw!

Uncle Mac yelled, "June get the hell out of here and take them mothafuckas with you!"

June yelled back, "You thought I forgot but I didn't forget how you beat me almost to death after raping me. I actually liked yo ass, Mac!"

Uncle Joe yelled, "Bitch is yo ass crazy?! My brother ain't rape nobody! Yo ass was just here earlier drinkin' up every damn thang. And now yo ass talkin' about somebody rapin' you. Bitch please! Git the hell out of here!"

June snapped back, "I know I didn't say nothin' earlier cause I just remembered after I fell and bumped my head. I drink a little too much at times, but I know what happened to me when we were younger."

Mama said, "June, you got it all wrong. Mac ain't raped nobody!"

"Shut the hell up Hope, ain't nobody talkin' to you!" June yelled as she pulled out a gun.

Uncle Mac calmly told June to put away the gun and tried to explain that she was mistaken. June tried to fire the gun at Uncle Mac, but once again she was drunk, she missed. Each of our purple stones began to light up. The fire that was so familiar in my uncle's eyes began to ignite.

Mama spoke these words:

**"Time stands still once again to open for the past**

**May our ancestors protect us this night as this spell is cast**

**For the truth will be revealed once more**

**All the lies will be no longer stored"**

Thunder and lightning tore open the sky. Which meant, shit was about to go down again.

June said, "Get 'em, throw some chicken bones at 'em. Y'all ain't the only mothafuckas that know voodoo."

One man walked up to Uncle Mac and blew some kind of dust in his face. But had a puzzled look when Uncle Mac didn't react.

Uncle Joe laughed and said as his eyes lit up, "No this mothafucka didn't!"

Next thing I know, Uncle Mac hit the man so hard, he landed halfway across the yard unconscious. In slow-motion, June was still tryin' to shoot the gun at all of us. The sorry ass men she convinced to come with her ran the minute the spell was broken. June just stood there as she cried.

Mama said, "June you know damn well my brotha ain't raped you or nobody else for that matter. What in the hell would make you say something like that? We all grew up together. That's why you need to stop drinkin'!"

"Ask him! Ask him!" June yelled.

"I don't have to ask Mac nothin'! Do you really think I'm gonna ask my brotha if he raped you let alone someone else?! June you are a drunk and everyone knows it. Most of the time people pay you know mind. But now you're talkin' bout accusing Mac of rapin' yo ass! Hell Naw! Have you noticed that you're just standing here and can't move?"

June nodded her head saying' yes and then said, "Voodoo, I know y'all mothafuckas, sorry my fault, you folks use voodoo. I knew even Ms. Thelma used it. I loved Ms. Thelma. Is Ms. Thelma gonna come up out of the grave? Ms. Thelma told me if I didn't stop drinkin', she was gonna come back for me."

Is this woman serious, I was thinking to myself? Did this lady asked if Gram-T was comin' out of the grave? I done heard it all. I'm surprised Mama didn't slap her.

Mama said calmly, "No June we don't use voodoo. But we use something else. Because of all the drinkin' and smokin' you got your facts all mixed up. Do you even remember how you got that scar on your forehead?"

"Ah, yeah runnin' from Mac in the woods that night when he was beatin' me! Say it, Mac!" June demanded.

Uncle Joe jumped in and said, "See that's where yo ass is wrong! Mac ain't gonna hit a woman. Now me on the other hand, if you hit me, I may have to lay hands on yo ass."

Mama placed both hands on June's temple.

June got scared and asked, "What in the hell are you doin', Hope?!"

Mama spoke these words,

**"By the winds of the night**

**And through the fire that burns bright**

**The past that should be dead**

**May it come forth in your head."**

June stood there with a glazed look in her eyes as she began to rub her forehead. She began to remember as she whispered, "Eddie" while tears ran down her cheeks. You could tell she was embarrassed. She held her head down in shame.

Scared to look Uncle Mac in the eyes. She mumbled, "I don't know how I got you confuse with that bastard. "

"Shit, I do. Yo ass drink too damn much!" Uncle Joe interrupted once again.

"June, you can't go around accusing people of crazy stuff and think they just gonna walk away. That can get you killed, girl." Auntie said.

June stood there looking pitiful. It was hard to feel sorry for her after accusing my Uncle of rape, thinkin' Gram-T was gonna rise up out the grave and tryin' to shoot us. Auntie pulled Mama aside and asked if they should do another mind sweep to clear June's memory. Uncle Joe agreed and said we didn't need any more crazy relapses from June.

"Naw we don't need to do nothin'. Trust me, June will be fine. She'll go home and drink herself to sleep and won't remember anythin'. Folks don't listen to half the stuff June says anyway. Just send her on her way." Uncle Mac said.

By this time, the police were coming around the back with their guns drawn, saying they got a call that June was kidnapped. But when the police arrived, all they saw was us sitting around the fire pit and June drinking a cup of tea Auntie made. I don't know if it was exactly tea or not. But June had a different demeanor. Mama kindly explained that June had too much to drink as well as her un-

*Blood, Secrets and Lies 2 The Grave*

invited guests, who were told to leave. June agreed quietly and the police took her home.

"Hell, I need a drink." Uncle Max said.

We all agreed. Auntie went into the shed and dusted off this bottle covered with layers of dust.

I asked, "Ah, did you find that under the shed with all that dust and dirt? You sure that's somethin' to drink?"

"This is one of Papa's bottle of moonshine. Not that cute fancy stuff y'all buy in the stores. Papa was the best when it came to fishin' and makin' whiskey. On Friday night, he and a few of his buddies would gather outback fryin' fish and drinkin' his homemade moonshine." Auntie said.

Uncle Mac got some cups and poured all of us some of the whiskey. But he only gave me and Sandra a sip.

He said, "I know y'all are grown, but y'all ain't that grown."

# Chapter Seven

## Flashback

Today I prayed for a better outcome at Uncle Joe's. It will be just the family, no neighbors, friends, and no Ms. June. Daddy planned on grillin' some ribs, chicken, Boudin sausage and fish. While the ladies were makin' the sides. The sides consisted of a little bit of everyone's favorites like baked beans, corn on cob, shrimp and crawfish rice casserole, mac & cheese, lima beans, peach cobbler, caramel cake with pralines on top just to name a few. We decided on watchin' old home movies, playin' cards and charades. Uncle Mac's sons, Junior, Tim, and Sean had never seen any of the home movies. I loved seeing Gram-T and Grandpa Jerry along with their siblings when they were younger and enjoyin' life. Seeing family members that instilled values in us that are no longer here makes me a little sad. As we were hanging the movie sheet in front of the shed, Uncle Joe mentioned the rules.

He said, "No talkin', standin' up in front, and no laughin' at the fashion either."

"Just start the movie, Joe. Does anyone wants any more dessert before we start?" Mama said.

We all agreed that we were stuffed and just wanted to watch the films. We were halfway through an old movie with Gram-T and her sisters, Mama started to cry. Daddy held her hand. We were all starstruck when we saw Aunt Faith. She was so beautiful. It was like watching this Angel on screen. She had the prettiest blue eyes. She puts you in the mindset of a young Lena Horn or Dorothy Dandridge, very elegant and classy. I'm sorry I never got the chance to meet her. Willie, Sandra's younger brother started to play some dance music to change the mood. So we started the Soul Train line. Daddy ended up my partner. He tries to do the latest dances but has no luck. But he's fun to watch. Mama danced with Uncle Mac doin' the bump. Now my Uncle Joe can dance his ass off. He ended up with Sandra doing the robot. We were outside playin' spades, dominoes and reminiscing on old times until the sun went down. Eric and the fellas went into the house to watch a game. The rest of us just set outside in the old families rockin' chairs under the stars. Of course I got the same question, "When are you and Eric gonna start a family?" I say the same thing, "When it happens you will be the first to know." People don't understand what Eric and I went through after his stabbing. So we're taking our time. But we're both ready. So when it happens, I'll be overjoyed. Everyone started slowly goin' in the house except for me.

"I should have known you would be the last one out here by yourself. Even as a kid you would rock for hours at night by yourself. What have you been thinkin' bout, Cher?" Uncle Joe asked.

I responded, "The stars. I always thought each star was an ancestor lookin' down at me. So I would try to guess what they were thinkin'. I know that sounds strange."

"Naw it don't. You're probably right." He said.

"Uncle Joe, have you done anything you regretted that you think the ancestors or God would be disappointed in?" I asked.

He laughed then looked at me and saw I was serious. He cleared his throat and said, "Ree there are a few things I could have done differently but regret, naw. Some stuff I did, I gotta answer for, but I'm takin' that to the grave."

"Like what?" I asked.

He said, "If I tell ya, I won't be takin' it to the grave. Why you askin'? Did you do somethin'?"

"Naw, I was just wondering. You don't talk a lot about yourself now or when you were younger. What were you like as a kid? Were you always confident with swag?" I asked.

"Ree, what you see is what you get. But I wasn't always so smooth. When I was a kid, I had a stutterin' problem. The kids teased me, but they didn't bother me much. But this one white teacher, Mr. Wood would always tell me I wouldn't be nothin' but a "Dumb Nigga". His problem wasn't that I stuttered but I stuttered, and I was smart and stood up for myself. He tried to put me in a special education class, but I refuse to go. So mama came to school and demanded for the teacher to be reprimanded. But back in those days, blacks had to know their place. So nothing was done to the teacher. Mama continued to help me with my stutterin'. Years later after I graduated, I saw this same bastard. Mac and I took over the family diner and we were expanding the restaurant. So we were taking bids from different contractors. When I saw his

*Blood, Secrets and Lies 2 The Grave*

name on the list of contractors, I reminded Mac what he did to me. Mac asked me what I wanted to do. I wanted to put him down like a wild dog. But Mac reminded me of the consequences of our actions. So he came by one evening. He didn't recognize us or our name. I offered him a cold beer because it was the end of the day, and it was hot as hell. We showed him the land that we purchase next to the diner. He wanted our business so bad, that he outbid the other contractors right there on the spot. Mac and I started to laugh. Then this fool started laughing and didn't know why. He stopped when I said, "Dumb Nigga."

He paused and said, "Pardon me?"

I repeated myself again, "Dumb Nigga."

He had no idea what I was talkin' bout. So Mac brought the night early. The storm clouds hovered over us. That shit wasn't funny then. He looked into my eyes, and I shared with him the good old days. He tried to leave and started babblin' about what made him that way. But what he didn't know was, that Mac and I have the gift of sight. We can see inside your mind to see the truth. This mothafucka was lyin'. He started to choke without me layin' hands on him. Mac had to calm me down and keep me from killin' him. He pissed on himself and begged for mercy. I told him, "Here's what yo ass gonna do Sammy boy. You gonna sell your construction business to Mr. Bill, the one you have been stealing his clients for years because he's black." At first, he said, "Hell no." But as he began to choke more while being held up in the air, that got his attention. I told him he had twenty-four hours to sign over his business or we would come after his wife, Nora and his two kids."

I asked, "Did he sign the papers to Mr. Bill?"

Uncle Joe said, "Not at first. He didn't think fat meat was greasy. I went by his place the next night. He was in his office loading bullets in a gun. He tried to shoot me but that didn't work. This time I did actually grab him by the throat and held him up in the air. He saw the fire in my eyes and family mark on my hand light up. He started yellin' for help. I silenced him. I had some papers drawn up and he signed them along with a note to Mr. Bill, sayin' he wanted to make things right. The last thing I had him sign, was a suicide note. He begged for his life. I told him I wasn't going to take his life."

"Uncle Joe, did you kill him?" I was scared to ask.

"I just walked out the door. Then I heard a gunshot go off. You should be more careful when someone offers you somethin' to drink, even a cold beer. C'mon let's go inside." Uncle Joe finished.

I said, "Yeah that's something to regret and to take to the grave."

Uncle Joe reply, "I didn't say I regretted it."

# *Chapter Eight*

# Fire

*S*aid I would never do another dead client's hair again unless it was my immediate family. But Tiffany asked me to do her sorority line sister, Mia's grandmother's hair. The family lived in Decatur Georgia, which wasn't too far. Tiffany even offered to go to the funeral home to help. We were meeting the family to get an idea of how they wanted their grandmother's hair styled. We pulled up to the funeral home, it looked like a player's club convention in the parking lot. I saw everything from, Cadillacs pumped up on rims, Jerri curls and big gold chains with the teeth to match. Tiffany's Sands introduced us to the entire family. The first aunt brought me a blue sequence minidress and blue 6-inch-high heel shoes. I had to explain to her that I was only doing her hair. The other had a big bag of makeup that she got from the dollar store.

"Here y'all, is her activator." The uncle said.

"What's activator?" Tiffany asked with a silly look on her face.

The uncle reply, "Gal you funny. It's to keep her hair nice and shiny. So it don't get dry."

"Ok, y'all give them a chance to get and to see Queenie first. Y'all wait out here." Mia said

The reason I don't do dead clients is because it's too much pressure trying to make them look like their old selves. And of course, the fact that they are dead. I was put on the spot, when I was asked to do Eric's mom hair when she died. I was a mess. I ran to the bathroom to throw up. I couldn't say no. Her hair turned out beautiful, but she had a nice grade of hair, to begin with. The funeral director was so impressed with my work she asked if I would be interested in doing other clients. I told her I appreciate the offer but that's not what I do.

Tiffany, Mia, and I walked into the room where her grandmother was lying. Tiffany and I stayed back to give me some time first with her grandmother. Mia quietly just stared at her with no words. She leaned down and gave her a kiss while whispering something in her ear. She motioned for us to come over.

*Blood, Secrets and Lies 2 The Grave*

"Queenie, these are my sorors and they are gonna make you look like the queen you are. Okay, Renée, she is the showstopper of the family. So she gotta look ghetto fabulous. She likes the smooth finger waves on the side, spiked hair on top with blonde color and her curls in the back. Don't forget her baby hair slicked down. I got her gel, activator, and color spray. I even got some extra if you ain't got none." Mia said.

I was speechless. But I didn't want to offend her.

"Sands we got you. Renée is the best at what she does. Just go and be with your people outside. We'll take care of Ms. Queenie. Renée got her products and styling tools. Save your products. Maybe someone else can keep 'em." Tiffany said

Mia high-fived both of us and left.

"Don't you charge extra for multiple hairstyles in one? So what's your plan cause I know you ain't doing all that shit. I know you hate finger waves. Tiffany laughed.

I just stared quietly at this beautiful dark-skinned woman that had a beautiful chocolate complexion. She looked at peace with no regrets. To be called, "Queenie or Queen" by all, says a lot about her. So I must give her a hairstyle that represents a queen minus the ghetto fab suggestions. Her hair was already washed and blow dried. Her hair was thick. So I decided to cut it short on the sides to give a wave effect. For the top of her hair, I put a little bend on the end, so it looks spiked like as I pulled the strands apart. I tapered the bottom and left two soft hanging curls along the nape of her neck. I lightly spray the spikes with the gold hairspray and gently laid her edges down.

"Ree, I can do her makeup. She doesn't need a lot. I'll just shape her eyebrows, brush on her foundation followed by a finished powder that they have right here in the morgue. Just a little eyeliner on top of the eyelids. I can use the gold hairspray on her eyelids. What?! It ain't like it'll burn her eyes. And finish it with this fuchsia dollar store lipstick with a touch of the gold hairspray on top. Trust me, Ree." Tiffany said

When we were done, I couldn't believe my eyes. Mrs. Queenie looked fabulous. Maybe I do need to consider doing this. Who knows? Tiffany went to get Mia and her aunts.

"Ah damn, y'all did that shit! Hell yeah." The other aunt said loudly.

"She needs mo gold eyeshadow on, don't she?" The cousin said.

Mia said, "Naw! Leave her alone. We don't need you messin' stuff up. She's perfect. Now that lipstick is on point. Which one did you use? I'll be using that for myself."

Tiffany replied, "Ah you can get it at the dollar store."

Ms. Queenie's three brothers came in.

One uncle said, "Ah shit, baby girl you look good. ReeRee and Taffy did hooked yo ass up. Y'all do mens?

"Do we do dead mens? "Tiffany mocked with a smirk.

The uncle said as he removed his Fedora hat, "Do y'all cut mens hair? I need someone who can set my waves and put some color on it."

As I look at his shoulder length hair and bald spot on top, I was tryin' to figure out where do you put finger waves.

I politely said, "I'm sorry uncle, no I don't service men."

"Okay, well thanks ReeRee and Taffy for hookin' up my baby sistah. Here y'all go." The uncle said.

He handed me three, one-hundred-dollar bills. Shit, maybe I should consider doing this for a living. For three hundred dollars you can call us, ReeRee and Taffy anytime.

Tiffany leaned over and said, "Ah ReeRee I need one of those bills."

"Yeah, you did do her makeup flawlessly, Taffy." I said.

For the next few days, I couldn't stop laughin' and callin' Tiffany, Taffy. But something that wasn't funny, was that money and that for doing Mrs. Queenie's hair and makeup. This funeral director said I could make some nice quick money because all the client's hair already been washed and dried. Even Tiffany could do their makeup. Tiffany does a lot of my client's makeup. That's becoming a big moneymaker also. When we were kids, Tiffany would put mama's makeup on Leah, and it looked just as good as the cover girls on the magazine. And now that I got a little bit more comfortable in the morgue since tryin' to find Tony, I'm going to seriously think about this.

Finally, love was in the air once again in Georgia. Kim and I were working from sunup to sundown. We both had several weddings to style for. Eric called and said he was picking up dinner and asked if I could get off work early. We needed some quality time. When I got home, the music was playing and the food was on the table. Eric just got out of the shower. He looked good standing there in his underwear. Shit, he looked good standing there butt ass naked. We both were starving cause it got quiet at the table.

"I got you some dessert." He said.

"You know I have a sweet tooth. Whatever you got is fine with me. What did you get?" I asked.

He said nothing. Just smile slowly looking down between his legs. We both laugh.

Sometime around 2 AM. There was a hard knock at the door. Eric came into the bedroom to tell me it was Kim and the salon caught on fire. I couldn't believe it. I asked if anyone was hurt. Kim said the salon was closed and no one was hurt. We got dressed to go see the damage.

When we got there, the firetrucks were packing up. The police grilled me as though I had something to do with it. My salon was destroyed! And I'm being treated like a criminal. My head was pounding. Eric was trying to keep me calm and Kim was trying to tell the police we had nothing to do with the fire. This shit was pissin' me off. I had to keep explaining I had no reason to burn down my salon. Eric had no reason to burn down the salon or Kim. No, we didn't have any enemies. No, we didn't owe anyone money. Why not assume something else, like bad electric wiring. I couldn't help but notice a glare from across the street. I could have sworn I saw a purple flash of light. I tried to take a second look, but the officer was giving me his card to call if I had any questions. He told me to come by the station in the morning for a complete copy of the report. I put my fake smile on and thanked him. I looked across the street again and there was no one there. I asked if I could go in, but the fire chief said no it was still too dangerous.

By the time Eric and I got home, we were dead on our feet. We were able to squeeze in two hours of sleep. I had to call my clients to reschedule them at my other salon. I thank God I own another salon that I can work out of. I told Kim she can use the empty booth at the other salon as well. Mama and Daddy were relieved that no one was hurt. The phone was glued to my ear for the next few days, talking with family, insurance company, clients in

*Blood, Secrets and Lies 2 The Grave*

my financial planner. Teresa called to check to see if I needed help with anything.

Eric asked me what I plan to do, rebuild, different location or different business altogether. I honestly hadn't thought about it yet. Part of me was still in shock. He told me I had plenty of time to figure things out. While we were talking the doorbell rang. It was the detective from the police station.

Detective Smith said, "According to the fire inspector, the fire started in the supply closet. It seemed to be ignited by something like a Molotov cocktail or firebomb. But that was just an idea. They're still not certain how the fire ignited. So I ask you again, do you owe anyone money? Did you get into an altercation with someone? Did you sleep with someone who wasn't your spouse? Or what about a disgruntled employee or client. You pissed somebody off and they ain't playin'.

I said, "Detective Smith as I told you before, NO! I have no idea who would do this."

Detective Smith looked at Eric and said, "What about you? This could have been someone trying to get back at you as well. Even family members can do crazy stuff if you give 'em a reason."

Eric said calmly, "No. We don't owe anyone money. You can check our bank accounts. I go to work and maybe the gym after. I keep to myself, then I come home. Do you have any leads or suspects other than us?"

Detective Smith replied, "No but I'll still be in touch. Thank you for your time."

The next few days I had to lay low. I knew I would be watched by the police and whoever set the fire. But I still had every intention of finding out who did this. Mama invited all of us over just to hang out while the men go fishin'. It just so happens that my Uncles were here in town. They will travel anywhere to go fishin'. Eric and I got dressed and headed to Mama's. It was good that my Uncles were here. It's like having extra protection. Whoever set this fire has a serious vendetta against me. So I have to be careful, not just for my sake but for the whole family's sake.

When we got to the house, they were already in the backyard relaxing after a big breakfast. The fishing equipment was already in the trucks. They were just waiting on Eric. Eric isn't really a fisherman like my family, but he tries. I don't care what occasion when my family comes around, I can't help but get emotional. It's nice to scroll through the family photos and reminisce. I think back to the summers in New Orleans with Gram-T, Grandpa Jerry, and the whole family, pla-yin' church in Gram-T's backyard, double dutch in the streets and jacks on the sidewalk. The elders were no longer with us. But now Mama and 'em are the elders now. It is true what they say, "The young shall become the old." That's why I try to enjoy every minute of my family. Eric kissed me and headed out with the fellas. As Uncle Joe and Uncle Mac walked past me, they both kissed me and said, "No worries, Cher." As they walked out of the door, I saw the symbols on their hands light up. That was the first time my scar was glowing. Tiffany and Leah arrived with the carmel cake in hand. They know that's mine and Daddy's favor-ite cake. As we were looking through the family photo albums, Uncle Joe brought an album that was in Gram-T's old trunk. Mama never seen these albums. We were going through the family photos tryin' to figure out who possibly wants to harm me. Tiffany came across an old photo of Gram-T and her sisters outside. All of them smiling except Aunt Hope on the end.

"Why is Aunt Hope frowning like y'all made her take this picture? Here's another photo of them except Gram-T is standing next to Aunt Hope. But their arms aren't around each other." Leah asked.

Tiffany said, "You see there is some tension between the two of them. There are several other photos of Aunt Hope in the background not participating, not smiling and arms folded. She's beautiful but she looks so angry."

I asked, "Mama how come you never seen these albums? What's wrong with Aunt Hope?"

"Honestly I don't know why these photos were put away. I don't know much about Aunt Hope at this point in her life. She was young. That will be a question for Mac or Joe." Mama said.

We came across a picture of a baby, but mama didn't know who she was. We took a break from photos. We dove into the carmel cake. Mama took this time to explain to Leah and Tiffany about the men in our family and their special gifts.

A few hours later the men were back, asking us to come out to the back to see what they caught. I was surprised to see this huge catfish that took up all the space in the one cooler.

Eric asked, "Who's gonna clean and gut all of these fish that were caught?"

We all pointed to him as we laughed. Then Daddy said he has a friend that he pays to do that. But if we were back in New Orleans with my Uncles, they would clean their own fish. Friday night at the family diner would be packed because it was Friday fish fry dinners on the menu.

Eric went to work early. I had to run some errands. We were having the family over our house for dinner while Uncle Mac and Uncle Joe were still in town. It would also give us a chance to figure out who burned down the salon. Daddy was gonna smoke some chicken and Boudin sausage Uncle Joe brought from New Orleans. We were all pitch in to do the sides. Daddy had his camera taking pictures of everyone. That was kinda his thing. He didn't like pictures from the phones. He is still old-fashioned. Eric blessed the food and we dug in. We laughed, joked, and reminisce about the good old days. That's why daddy loves photo albums. Cell phones come and go. But photos last throughout generations.

The fellas were outside on the patio drinking and relaxing. Mama started going through the old albums again. Uncle Mac came back in to get some more poundcake when Mama asked him about the pictures and album.

"Mac, why did Mama have this album put away? I've never seen these photos till now. There are pictures of Aunt Hope and others. Why didn't Aunt Hope come around? She was like a ghost." Mama asked.

Uncle Mac set down with a slice of cake and said, "There was always tension between Mama and Aunt Hope. I'm surprised Mama named you after her. These pictures were taken at the last family get-together that Aunt Hope came to. Yeah, she looked pissed on these pictures because she didn't want to take them. She and Mama got into some huge argument. I don't know what they were fightin' about. I was inside the house. I came outside when Uncle James was holding Aunt Hope. Aunt Vera was holding Mama back from fightin'. You know you don't get in grown folks' business. All the kids were told to go inside. But me and Joe were standing by the screen door tryin' to listen. We could hear nothin' because of too much cryin' and yellin'. As far as this baby picture, I don't know who this is. Sorry I couldn't help. Anyway, Ree, be careful. I and Joe are leaving tomorrow instead of the weekend. Joe does talk with Pat and she's on her way to the ER. Her blood pressure is high again. So we're gonna head out in the morning. But if you need me to stay, I can."

"No Uncle Mac, I'm good. You guys can go see about Aunt Pat and give her our love from Georgia." I said.

I couldn't sleep at all. So I called Leah and said I was on my way with some of the ashes, along with Gram-T's gumbo pot and herbs. When I got there, Tiffany was already waiting.

"You couldn't sleep either? We need to find out who did this shit and put an end to 'em." Tiffany said.

I reminded her we're not murderers. Whoever did this wasn't trying to kill anybody. Otherwise they would have set the fire during the day while we had clients. They were sending a warning of some kind.

"Yeah, a warning that is costing you a lot of money." Tiffany said.

The three of us did a family revealing spell using Gram-T's gumbo pot. We mix the ashes from the salon fire with different herbs. We removed our purple family stones from our jewelry, my ring, Leah's bracelet, and Tiffany's necklace. We placed them in the pot positioning them in a triangle. Next, we placed the ashes in the center. Immediately the ashes and herbs began to burn. Water was poured in the pot slowly and we waited. We looked in the pot to see if a vision had appeared. At first, there was an image of an older man holding a Bible walking away from someone. Next, we saw three women of different ages. We didn't know them, and they weren't in the photo albums. We were all clueless. Was this man related to the ladies? Or was he related to us? This didn't help us at all. Tiffany suggested going to the salon and doing the spell there.

By the time we got to the salon, it was around 1 AM. It was quiet on the streets. Tiffany pried the wood off the back door. Something didn't feel right. One of my gifts was, when something was wrong, I will get these headaches. I don't know if that's a gift or curse. It felt like someone was watching. Whoever set the fire was close by.

Leah said, "Whoever did this, is a part of our family?! Look at the wall, there is a symbol on it if you look closely. The same family symbol on the web of our hands. I picked up some of the ashes and threw them at the wall and said,

**"Ashes within ashes, dust all over dust**

**Hate, harm, pain, and broken trust**

**From our ancestors from the past**

**To our descendants we'll teach to cast**

**Reveal this night the hate and intent**

**Show the heart and what was meant"**

On the wall showed a clear vision of Gram-T and Aunt Hope younger and arguing over a man. Aunt Hope accused Gram-T of liking him. Gram-T was only warning her of that backwoods preacher who was married to stay away from him. But Aunt Hope already knew that but still loved him. Aunt Hope was pregnant by him. Their father John told Aunt Hope she couldn't bring in some bastard child in his house. The sorry preacher denied everything even the baby. Aunt Hope argued with her father, that they helped Thelma or Gram-T when she got pregnant with Faith and the only reason, they helped her was because she was pregnant by a white man. That's when their father slapped Aunt Hope. Aunt Hope ran off with Gram-T chasing behind her. So the baby in the photo belonged to Aunt Hope. The old photo of all the sisters was years later when Hope came to one of the family get-togethers demanding something. But it wasn't clear what she wanted.

"What did Aunt Hope want? This is crazy." Tiffany said.

Leah asked as we walked outside, "But what does all this have to do with you and the salon being burnt down?"

"Oh I can answer that." An unknown voice said in the parking lot.

"Who are you?! Leah asked.

She responded, "Isn't it obvious?"

"If it was obvious, she wouldn't have asked!" Tiffany snapped back.

"Wait a minute you came into my salon a while ago. Asking about Jonathan. Is this shit all about his ass?!" I demanded.

She said calmly, "Naw never met the guy. That was just an excuse to come to the salon to size you up. The name Grace doesn't ring a bell?"

"Look cut the shit, who are you and who is Grace?! And what the hell that gotta do with me and my salon? Did you do this shit?! As I started walking towards her.

"I'm Tasha, the daughter of Grace and granddaughter to Hope Sullivan who was banished from the family like an outcast! "She yelled.

I stopped in my tracks and saw a purple glow coming from her shirt. She pulled out the necklace which revealed our family stone. She was one of us. But why the chaos?

"My grandmother Hope was treated like the disgraced black sheep of this family. She made a mistake that everyone held over her head. But your grandmother, Thelma did the same damn thing way before my grandmother. But the family helped your grandmother. My grandmother went back asking for forgiveness from her parents. But she was too late. Their mama died the year before and nobody told her. And to top it off the family stones for her descendants were not given to her." Tasha said.

Tiffany yelled, "What the hell that has to do with us?! My sister salon?! This is some old family vendetta about my grandmother?! Guess what, she's dead too! If truth be told I heard your grandmother and mother did the unthinkable against our ancestors and God. Maybe that's why they were banished from the family. To raise the dead is forbidden."

I demanded again, "What the hell do you want with me?!"

Tasha pointed to me and said, "Your grandmother was given the remaining family stones instead of my grandmother. I want what's ours! Your ring belongs to me!"

"Are you crazy, all this over some damn jewelry that you think belongs to you?! So you decide to burn down my shop to get my attention?! Well here I am! Come get this ring if you wanted so bad! I must warn you it won't be easy!" I told her.

Tasha said, "Oh I'm not alone. You gonna give me what's owed to me you stuck up ass bitch!"

Out of nowhere this man, about 250 pounds, tall, brown skin with no expression on his face appears. He didn't say anythin'. This mothafucka starts walkin' towards me. Tiffany cast a strong wind to knock him down, but he didn't budge. His eyes were dark as midnight then turning to red flames. It was like he was possessed. He picked up a handful of dirt and threw it up in the air. It was like a tornado hit us. We all were knocked to the ground. He grabbed me by my neck and held me up in the air with one hand. He tried to grab the necklace with the other hand, but I sent a bolt of lightning through his body that threw him back. Fire lit up in all three of our eyes. Tasha conjured up a fire that surrounded us. As the fire came closer

*Blood, Secrets and Lies 2 The Grave*

to us, with one wave of Leah's hand she brought a tsunami down to eliminate the flames. The big man was still determined to come for me again. With one stomp of his foot, the earth opened up. What the hell! Two faceless creatures crawled out. I couldn't believe my eyes. It seemed as though our powers were useless against Tasha. The creatures held each of us and began strangling us. Tiffany had passed out. I tried everything but these creatures were stronger than us. I started feeling faint, but I was determined to hold on and fight. Just as I began to close my eyes, I see two more figures coming our way with fire in their eyes. Shit, it's over! But suddenly the creatures began to holler in agony and loosen their grip around our necks. I look up and see Uncle Mac and Uncle Joe. How is this possible? They had these knives that were on fire. They look like they were moving in slow motion towards us. I regained my strength. Uncle Joe and Uncle Mac were both fighting two of the creatures. The third creature was ours. Leah started a fire in her hand. The creature obviously feared the fire and ran into the woods in the back. I reached into the earth and pulled up branches and called on our ancestors for help. The wind blew hard, the leaves open a pathway clear to the last creature bound to a tree by branches. It had the appearance of a young man without a face covered with dirt. This is not of God.

I said these words,

**"Fire to the night and open thy sight**

**Reveal from the grave who has awoken and made into a slave"**

A face appeared with his creature so innocent. The face of a young man unaware of what was going on.

I asked, "Who are you?"

He responded, "I'm one of many of the dead. My name was Paul Jr. Why have I been called from my slumber?"

Tiffany demanded, "You've been brought back from the dead and you don't know why or who did it?"

"All I know was, my time in this world was short as well as my father and brother. We had been brought back to do one's bidding. But the price for her will be too high. I see you have the blood of our ancestors in your eyes. So you could not at all be our enemy." He said.

*Blood, Secrets and Lies 2 The Grave*

I put him back in his slumber. We ran back to where Tasha and her Uncles were left fighting. When we arrived, the creatures and Tasha were bound by branches. I was so glad to see my Uncles.

"How on earth did you guys end up here? We thought you left to go back to New Orleans." I asked

"We knew whoever was watchin' you was watchin' us, so we had to make it look real. We could feel somethin' was wrong and so did yo Mama. Someone was using death spells again and that's forbidden." Uncle Mac said.

I look at Tasha and said, "All this for a ring and revenge for people who are no longer living?!

"It wasn't just them. My Uncle Paul and his two sons were killed in a car accident! We didn't see none of y'all at the funeral!" Tasha yelled back.

"Wait we didn't know about your uncle and cousins until after the fact. Aunt Hope had nothing to do with the family for years. You can't hold us accountable for what took place with the elders." Uncle Mac said.

Tasha clapped back, "What if it was your son in that wreck that died along with his two sons?! If you could bring them back, would you?"

"We can't play God! You don't think I wanna see my Mama and my Pappa just for a second?! Uncle Joe said.

"Anyway, y'all, what are we gonna do with the walkin' dead and the crazy cuzin? Tiffany interrupted.

Uncle Joe said, "We have to return them back to the earth and put them to rest."

Uncle Mac went to his truck in the woods to get his shovel. He handed it to Tasha. He told her since she made this mess, she'll be cleaning it up. She refused at first. Until I told her if she didn't pick up the shovel, I'll take it and crack it upside her skull. When the grave was dug, Uncle Joe and Uncle Mac laid the bodies in. Tasha was handed the shovel to cover the grave. Uncle Joe with flames in his eyes sealed the grave closed. Never to be opened again.

Leah said, "Forgive us for your hurt, pain, suffering and lack of acknowledgment. May you have a peaceful rest for all of eternity. Amen."

"Bitch you cryin' after all yo ass did?! Tiffany yelled in Tasha's face.

We asked what our plans were for Tasha. Uncle Joe suggested beatin' her ass and tossing her over into a grave just for her.

I reminded him, she's family and we're not killer. Well distant family. He told me I sounded just like Mama as he pointed behind me. I turned around to find Mama walking towards us.

"Mama, what are you doing here?" Leah asked.

Mama said her stone change colors in the middle of the night. She knew something was wrong. A deadly spell was used she knew it wasn't us. She turned to Tasha and grabbed her hands. Mama has the gift of sight just with one touch she could see your life story.

"You are carrying so many burdens that are not yours. Your mother put so much hate and vengeance in you like her mother did. I'm sorry for the way Aunt Hope and her daughter Grace your mother, were treated by the family. Nothing changes that, not even calling on the spirit of the dead. Vengeance is an evil thing and causes you to do the unthinkable. That's why your mama and grandmother were banished because of a death spell they did to bring back your Uncle Paul. I see you have your mother's necklace with the family stone on." Mama said.

As Tasha tried not to cry, she said, "My mama and grandmother died brokenhearted. It was as though they didn't exist. Going to see Grandma Hope in the nursing home sitting in the corner always crying how sorry she was. Who made Emma and John God over them? Before mama died, she gave me her family stone necklace, but there wasn't one for my daughter! There will be no rose ceremony for my daughter!"

"Mama didn't hate Aunt Hope. I know their relationship was complicated. But Mama loved Aunt Hope and always talked about how she missed her. Mama would write her letters, but they were always returned. Except for the last year of Mama's life, Aunt Hope wrote back saying she loved her Big Sis Tilly as she was called only by Aunt Hope. Why do you think I was named after her?" Mama pleaded.

Tiffany interrupted once again, "Ah excuse me, this crazy B try to kill us using her uncle and cousins raised from the dead! What's the plan for her?!"

Mama said, "Mind sweep. We'll clear all the crazy and vengeful thoughts of this day, the past and the future. Unfortunately, it will erase some of the other good memories as well. Consequences of her actions. And I have to protect my family."

Mama placed a ring on Tasha's finger as Tasha began to sob. She told Tasha the family ring belonged to Aunt Vera, the oldest of the siblings. Tasha begged us not to do the mind sweep. She said how she regrets that she didn't know us and wished we could have gotten to know us. But Mama told her this was the only way. You just tried to kill us and then sayin' sorry. Me personally, I would have killed her ass and tossed her in a grave with her kinfolks, but we aren't killers. Or are we?

Weeks went by and no one spoke up that night. Leah came by several times just to talk but she was acting a little strange. So I decided to have a girl's night to get her to open up. Tiffany brought the drinks, Leah got the dessert and I ordered pizza. We had a ball. We all drank so much you have thought it was a bathroom break contest. We laughed like there was no tomorrow, we celebrated each other and celebrated our ancestors.

"Oh hell naw, who is pregnant?! There are two different pregnancy tests in the trashcan. And

I found the tests sticks in the cabinet underneath the sink with two different results." Tiffany yelled.

Leah said, "Well Carlos and I have been trying, but he's been doing a lot of traveling. So I took a test to see."

"Wait I took a pregnancy test as well." I said

"Ok one test is positive, and one test is negative. So you'll both have to do a second test to see to be sure." Tiffany said.

We all laughed and hugged from the excitement and the possibility of one of us being a mother. Tiffany was running around the room holding both pregnancy sticks in her hand. We were totally drunk.

"You know Ree, you may have to take two tests cause Jonathan got that gold tip. You know when he had yo honeypot and his golden tip for the last time, it made him go crazy when you decided to marry Eric. You know you need to take that shit to the grave." Tiffany laughed with her slurred speech.

As she and Leah were laughin', they suddenly stop with a strange look on their faces. I asked what was wrong. I turned around to see Eric standing in

*Blood, Secrets and Lies 2 The Grave*

the doorway coming home from a trip. With an awful look on his face. He heard everything Tiffany said.

"Oh shit party over." Tiffany said.

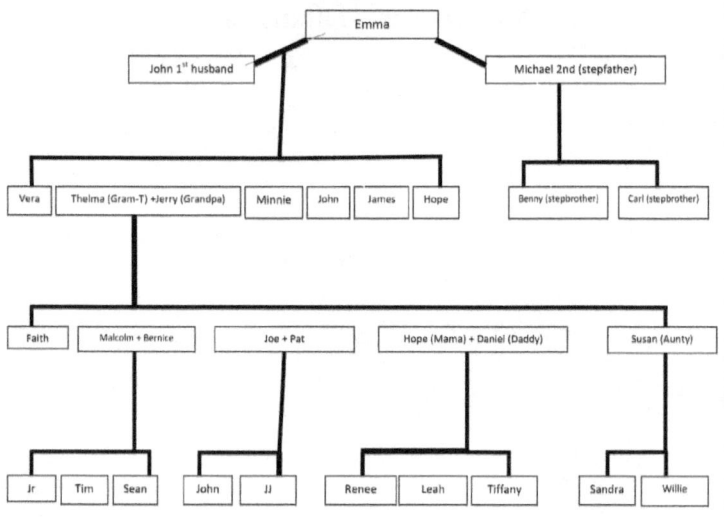

*Blood, Secrets and Lies 2 The Grave*

# Acknowledgments

I give my first acknowledgment to my heavenly father who has blessed me in countless ways. Thank you for providing me with wisdom, courage, strength and a great imagination. My mother, Renada "Nade" Howze, from day one taught me to never accept no, always go above and beyond and know your self-worth. My husband, Deshon Crayton who gave me my first set of ink pens when I said I wanted to write a book years ago, thank you for holding our family down. You're not big on words but you have a big heart. My two kids, Dallas and Elyse, who give me a reason to get up each day and be thankful, I want to encourage you both to love, laugh and always be your best. Remember you are loved and you are God's children. My sister, Maria C. Walker, thank you for loving me unconditionally and always pushing me to be my best according to God's will. My village, which consists of family, friends and neighbors who encouraged me throughout my journey, thank you. I thank you for all your prayers, guidance and keepin' it real talks.